D0595830

# Unbreak My Heart

*Rhonda McKnight*

*Rhonda McKnight*

Copyright © 2014 Rhonda McKnight Nain

God Cares Creations
P.O. Box 825
Ellenwood, GA 30294

All rights reserved. No part of this book may be reproduced in any form or by any means without prior consent of the author, excepting brief quotes used in reviews.

*This is a work of fiction. Any references or similarities to actual events, real people, living or dead, or to real locales are intended to give the story a sense of reality. Any similarity in other names, characters, places and incidents is entirely coincidental.*

ISBN:1500969214
ISBN-13:9781500969219

# Table of Contents

# Also by Rhonda McKnight

*Breaking All The Rules*
*Give A Little Love*
*An Inconvenient Friend*
*What Kind of Fool*
*A Woman's Revenge*
*Secrets and Lies*

# Dedication

For my son, Aaron McKnight...I pray God bless you with a lifetime of love and happiness.

# Acknowledgments

My readers – I wish I could list each and every one of you. Thank you for wanting my stories. Thank you also for waiting for them. Your emails and social media messages mean the world to me. They honestly keep me in front of the keyboard. Thanks also for the support and the reviews and spreading the word about my books. You really make this happen and I sincerely appreciate it.

Double love to my Facebook fans and group members. I appreciate you helping me flesh out ideas and taking the time to answer my research questions. You ladies in the Facebook – Rhonda McKnight Reading Group Rock!

Thanks to my author buddies Sherri Lewis, Tia McCollors, Tiffany L. Warren, Makasha Dorsey, Keleigh Criger-Hadley and Michelle Lindo-Rice for sharing your friendship, love, ears and shoulders…I'm so grateful that God has put you in my circle. I couldn't do this without you ladies.

More love to you, Sherri Lewis, you really, really, really and truly helped me put this book together. Girl, I love you. You're the best!

Janice Ingle - Even though I didn't make time to give this to you in advance I could hear your voice in my head saying, "Fix this," "That's not working", "I like it Rhonda." You are an awesome cheerleader and the spirit of your words is always with me.

To my sons, Aaron and Micah, thanks for putting up with my crazy writing world. What can I say…you two are an amazing gift from God.

*Love bears all things, believes all things, hopes all things, endures all things.* ~

1 Corinthians 13:7 (NKJV)

# Chapter 1

Fame comes at a price. Cameron Scott knew that better than anyone in her circle. One day you were "fab" and up. The next day you were down, walking the streets like a nobody with hashtag FAIL on your forehead. Fans, the media, friends and family talked about you on either end of the extreme, but you were invisible when you fell in the middle which was where Cameron was thought to be at this point in her career. Technically, she was actually at the bottom. Her fans just didn't know it yet.

Her contract with RAT Productions, Real American Television, was not going to be renewed. The show, similar to *The Chew* and *The View*, was replacing her. Her former boss was clear that she wasn't gritty enough for the sexy relationship chatter the show wanted to be known for nor had she brought authenticity to her feelings about what was going on in the featured guests' lives.

Authenticity to her feelings? He didn't want that. She'd never have a single good thing to say about a man. That was REAL. Every experience she'd ever had was negative, from the first man in her life to the most recent, her ex-fiancé, Doctor Rick Housely. If Cameron's thoughts could kill, he'd be resting in peace right now for announcing their break-up on television before he even told her. And she thought the folks sending break-up text messages were bad. Rick was such a jerk.

Housely was being interviewed on *Entertainment This Week*. When the interviewer asked him about their wedding date, he'd turned toward the camera with a sincerity that only those dreamy eyes of his could convey, and said, "I love you, Cameron, but I've searched my heart and prayed to God. I'm not ready for marriage. I hope you'll forgive me. I hope America will forgive me."

"Have you forgiven yourself?" the interviewer asked pushing the microphone further into his face. If she wasn't careful she'd hit that new cap he had on his front tooth and he'd jump on her.

Rick continued, "I have, because I know we're human and we make mistakes."

*Human.* Rick was barely that. *Ambitious.* That was more like it. And gay. Most definitely gay. If Cameron hadn't searched her heart, she'd shout that out to the entire world. But she had searched her heart and realized there was no reason to out Housely. Telling the world she'd accepted an engagement ring from a gay man was way down on the list of things she wanted to talk about. In fact, taking a ring from any man bottomed out a long time ago. And the truth was, she didn't love him. He'd lied about his sexuality and she'd lied about a few things of her own, so they were even.

"You look familiar," the taxi driver stated peering back at her.

Cameron noticed he'd been stealing glances every so often and she knew that peek. It was the, 'I've seen you on T.V.' look that she'd grown accustomed to getting. "Weren't you on that show with that guy?"

Cameron bit her tongue to keep from rolling her eyes and looked down into her purse. "Yep. *Is There A Saved Man In The House?*"

He snapped his fingers. "That's right. That's right. The dating reality show." He nodded his head a few times. She could tell he was smiling to himself like he'd figured it out on his own. "Sorry about the breakup."

Cameron looked up and forced a smile. "Thank you, but I've decided to assume it's for the best."

"Yes, but to put it on T.V. like that," he began. "I don't know how you Hollywood people do it. I don't think you could pay me a million dollars to be on T.V. with all those cameras following me and knowing all my private life."

Cameron took in his reflection in the rear-view mirror then sized up the condition of the grungy taxicab. *Couldn't pay him a million dollars?* She wondered what one had to pay him to get a haircut. People loved talking about what they wouldn't do for money until money was offered to them. "The show was mostly scripted."

"Script what?" he asked, his thick African accent getting stronger.

"There are writers. It's not all real. We're like actors." She waited a beat and then added. "It is entertainment you know."

"But people think it's real."

He had a valid point. And what people thought did matter. At least it did to her, but again, she wasn't outing Housely. Theirs was a relationship built on mutual need. Housely needed to launch his film career and she needed money, lots of it. That's why she'd auditioned for *Is There A Saved Man.*

Cameron never expected the on screen chemistry between her and Rick Housely to be so strong, especially since they didn't really click much off screen. Rick had set his eyes on her early and their cat and mouse game had captured the hearts of America; the last show being the one where Rick proposed and placed a huge diamond ring on her finger. Cameron reluctantly said yes. She knew she didn't love him. He didn't love her. And there was the matter of his questionable sexuality. She figured they would eventually break up. But even with all the anticipation of that moment, the show had been Cameron's lucky break in more ways than one. She had the diamond, but more importantly, she was a reality television star. Every talk show from *Good Morning America* to *Jimmy Kimmel* wanted to interview her and then out of those interviews came a weekly spot on *Real TV* to do a piece about Christian dating. Then she got her big break with RAT Productions for the *I Heart Show*. But she'd blown it. She'd blown it because she couldn't go the distance with the pretense.

Initially, she'd been fine with the dismissal. The show was stupid. She was sure she'd get another job. After all, she was Cameron Scott, America's reality show sweetheart. But meeting after meeting, after meeting there hadn't been a single offer. Not one call back. No interest in her at all. She was out of meetings and more importantly; she was out of time and money.

"401 Fifth Ave." The taxi driver's voice awakened her from her musing or was the blues a better way to describe her thoughts? Cameron was feeling sorry for herself. Sorry with a capital S.

She turned toward the passenger side window. Through the light misting of rain she glimpsed the aging building that housed the studio. She wrinkled her nose disapprovingly. Times Square, the heart of the theater district, was also the home to many of the country's T.V. studios. This building was less than a mile away from Times Square, but it felt like it was on the other side of the world. Hashtag FAIL. She couldn't help thinking it.

"Thanks." Cameron handed the cab driver the fare she couldn't afford and accepted the receipt he'd dutifully printed without asking. The cab ride was a splurge. It had been pouring down rain when she left home. She didn't want to wrinkle or stain her Armani suit traveling on the train in the rain. With dark glasses donned, she'd definitely be on the subway for the trip home.

Cameron opened the door and a blast of bone chilling wet air hit her like a brick. Manhattan in the winter…she hated it. She forced herself out of the warm taxi. Unbeknownst to her, she stepped right into an invisible hole in the asphalt. She gasped and twisted her body awkwardly to keep from falling. Fortunately, the door provided support otherwise she would have been sprawled out on the pavement.

"You okay, miss?" the driver called. His concern was genuine, but it was not appreciated. Cameron shook her head, turned to him and shot him the stink eye. He should have been more careful about where he'd stopped the passenger side door.

"I'm fine. No thanks to you!" She slammed the door like only a true New Yorker could. Glad that the heel of her Manolo shoe hadn't come off in the tussle, Cameron stepped up onto the sidewalk, smoothed her skirt and stopped breathing. She turned, the taxi whizzed down the street.

*Her attaché case.*

She'd left it on the backseat. Not only was it her favorite Coach bag, it also held her resume. How was she supposed to show up for the meeting without it?

Cameron swallowed, let out a long breath and counted to ten. "Pull it together. You know what this is about. You can't let it rock your confidence." She spoke the words out loud to herself, but thought inwardly, *if you don't get this job, you'll be homeless.*

Sufficiently motivated, she shook off thoughts of what she didn't have. She'd have to improvise. It wasn't the first time and as long as she was in the entertainment industry it surely would not be the last. But, she did want her bag back. Glad she noted the driver's name and taxi number, as she always did, Cameron tapped on her phone until she found the main number for Yellow Taxi, filed a missing item report and put in a request for the driver to call her to get it redelivered. She entered the building, showed security her appointment letter and rode the elevator to the third floor.

"I've never seen the righteous forsaken or his seed begging bread." She closed her eyes tight and whispered the verse from Psalm 37 over and over during the ride. The elevator doors opened. Cameron walked into a lobby full of women. Most of them were familiar: a couple of former stars from the *Housewives* franchise, one of the twins from that show about the sisters, she could never remember which was which, Tia and Tamera and one of the youngins' from the Kardashian clan. Her breath caught in her throat. *So much competition.* She wanted to repeat the scripture again, affirm what she knew by giving the Word power, but the only thing she could think as she approached the receptionist desk was maybe she wasn't one of the righteous.

\*\*\*

Five minutes into her meeting with the producer, she was sure she wasn't.

"I can email it as soon as I get home," Cameron replied to the question about her resume.

Myron Panther, the assistant producer, smiled tightly and said, "No need. I'm used to poor preparation, so I have the agents send the resume. The pictures are no big deal. I've seen you on camera."

Cameron fidgeted with her gloves under the table. "The show sounds very interesting. It sounds like a project I could really put my heart into." She pulled her bottom lips between her teeth. She couldn't believe she'd said something so incredibly dumb. She'd been fired from *I Heart* for not putting her heart into it.

Panther cocked an eyebrow. "I find it interesting that you were on a show about relationship talk and it didn't seem to be the best fit for you."

Cameron shifted in her chair. She had no doubt he knew the details of her dismissal. The audience had been polled a few times. Too many said, "They didn't feel her." She'd been hired to talk about things people loved, hence, the title for the show, *I Heart*. Those topics were food, fashion and celebrity gossip, but the show just seemed to focus on relationships: love, marriage, divorce and betrayal amongst celebrities and other famous people. She didn't want to talk about that every day and everyone knew it.

Cameron didn't want to appear too thirsty, but the reality of her situation was she was panting for a drink and soon she'd be starving for something to eat. She had no job, no money and a mountain of debt. She was going to be evicted from her apartment and the bank had already picked up her car. She owed her agent and best friend ten thousand dollars. The meager two thousand dollars she'd gotten when she pawned the last of her jewelry a few weeks ago was almost gone. As soon as she paid her cell phone bill tonight her bank account would be down to four hundred dollars. She had to get this job or she was going to have to start thinking crazy things about what she'd have to do if she didn't. And she did mean, cray-cray as in rob a bank. She shook her head to try and erase the image of her clothes on the street, raised her chin and decided to tell the truth, well part of it. "I could have done better on *Heart*. I'm properly motivated to do whatever it takes to make my next show a success."

Myron rolled his eyes. "So, are you saying the fifteen thousand a week they were paying you wasn't enough to motivate you?"

She swallowed, hard, and scrambled for a better answer. She couldn't think of anything, so instead of a lie, she decided to add more of the truth. "I was dealing with some personal problems. My grandmother had a stroke. The situation was grave and that distracted me, but I'm back on my game. I'm back to being the woman America fell in love with on *Saved Man.*"

She hoped the plug about the show would remind him of the stellar ratings. Three and a half million viewers a week on a cable network was a hit in today's rating game.

He nodded like he'd given that a quick thought and put his pen down. "We'll be in touch with your agent if we want you for the pilot." His face was completely unreadable, but Cameron had heard that twenty times in the last four months. Her heart sank.

She stood and exited Panther's office. The women that remained either rolled their eyes at her or gave the courtesy smile competing actors shared in waiting rooms. She held her head high and did what she did best; pretend it was all right. She went to the secretary's desk and stated, "I'll have my agent send that fax right over to Mr. Panther."

The young girl looked at her like she was crazy, but nodded.

"You have a good afternoon," Cameron continued. Then she turned toward the elevator. Relief engulfed her. The doors were standing open. She stepped inside and pushed the button several times, willing the doors to close before anyone else could join her, before anyone could see her lose it. She would not make it to the lobby before she broke down and cried.

# Chapter 2

The metal grate clanked beneath Jacob Gray's feet. Metal clanking, snow crunching, and the light whisper of the wind were the only sounds that could be heard for miles around. He loved the solace. He craved the peace.

"I can't believe I let you talk me into this."

Jacob smiled, pushed his snow goggles up and waited for his best friend, Ethan Wright to do the same. He looked out over the mountain they'd lifted to. Snowflakes the size of quarters melted against his hands and face. The floodlights on the slopes illuminated the dancing snow that floated to the ground.

"Any reason why we have to do this now?" Ethan asked.

This time Jacob laughed. "It's more fun at night, plus the snow will be coming down so thick in the morning we won't be able to see three feet in front of us."

Ethan groaned. "And none of that is a good reason to be up here at this time of night trying to whup your butt."

"This is practically a bunny slope," Jacob teased.

"Oh yeah, a thirteen hundred foot vertical drop is a bunny slope all right." Ethan's voice was filled with sarcasm.

Jacob was thoroughly amused. "Since when did you get so scary?"

"Since I got married and have something to look forward to. If Deniece saw this slope I wouldn't have to worry about killing myself going down it, she'd kill me before I could push off."

"That explains why you left her in New York."

Ethan shrugged. "I didn't leave her New York. I got run out of town. She's having a girlfriend's weekend with her sister and a few friends. They're going to the theatre, the ballet, eating out and shopping until the magnetic strip fades off the back of their credit cards."

Jacob laughed but it didn't reach his belly. He was happy for his friend's newfound love with his childhood sweetheart, but he couldn't help the twinge of jealously he always felt when he talked to Ethan or anyone, for that matter, who was truly in love. Lost love was the reason he was up on this mountain risking his life on a ski slope. "You needed an escape from shoe shopping, so you thought you'd hunt me down, huh?"

Ethan raised a gloved hand and scratched the side of his face. "I've missed you, but there's something you need to know. Since you've locked yourself up in that cabin with no phone, no internet and no television I didn't have a choice but to deliver the news in person."

Jacob waited a beat and asked. "Is it good or bad news?"

Ethan shrugged. "I think it's good, but it has the potential to go either way."

Jacob pulled his goggles down over his eyes. "If you're not sure, I'm inclined to not want to hear it until we're done."

Ethan pulled his goggles down too. "Well, let's get this over with."

"You can pass that hundred dollar bill in your pocket to me," Jacob added as he prepared to push off.

Ethan laughed. "You wish." The men counted to three before pushing off.

As with all skiing, it didn't take nearly as long to get down the hill as it did to get up it. The electric ride over long runs and bumps was a temporary fix for Jacob's depression. When he was on drifts like this, he had no choice but to focus on the trail. Before he knew it, the ride was over and his thoughts returned to his miserable life. He and Ethan were done, back at his cabin releasing their skis and catching their breath. It was time to learn what his friend had traveled so far to tell him.

"So, what is it?" Jacob asked pressing a crisp new hundred dollar bill into Ethan's waiting hand.

Ethan popped the bill a few times teasingly and put it in his top pocket. "Cameron is no longer engaged."

Jacob didn't know if there were any other words Ethan could have said that would have caused his heart to race the way it was racing now. It was a struggle, but he managed to say, "Go on."

"Her fiancé broke up with her a few weeks ago. He did it on television during an interview."

Jacob's jaw went slack.

"Nice guy, right? There's more." Ethan dropped his coat and hat into a nearby chair and paused for a beat. "I think she's in trouble."

Jacob frowned. "What kind of trouble?"

"You know she hasn't worked in a good while. She's being evicted from her apartment."

"How do you know…?" Jacob hesitated, answering his own question. "Deniece."

"A story broke on the news. She keeps up with all this stuff. Apparently someone at the city marshal's office leaked her name to the media."

"I knew she wasn't working, but eviction? How could she be broke?"

"She owes nineteen thousand dollars."

"Nineteen? Where does she live?"

"It's New York City, man." Ethan chuckled. "Anyway, she has a place on the upper Eastside. The rent is seven thousand a month." Ethan paused sticking his hands in his pockets and rocking back and forth on the heels of his boots. "So, now that you know this you need to come down from this mountain, my friend and fix it."

"You talk like it's that simple."

"I'm holding you to your word. After that T.V. guy proposed, I was the one who had to be your designated driver for a week. You said that if you ever had a chance with her you wouldn't blow it."

"She was just engaged. It's pretty obvious I'm the only one who hasn't moved on."

"Neither one of you have moved on. Getting a divorce is still on both of your to-do lists."

"Yeah, but she signed the divorce papers. She's ready to move on."

Ethan shook his head and eyed Jacob suspiciously. "Look. No excuses. You love the woman. Go tell her. If she doesn't feel the same then you can move on, but this perpetual state of what if..."

"It's not that simple. Things were really messed up."

"So, it was messed up. It's been almost five years. You've tried every dangerous sport known to man, slept with every woman that would have you and drank all the liquor you could handle and still... you're not over her, so you might as well go and try to make things right."

Jacob nodded.

"Look, I have to be honest. Some of what I've told you I learned through my wife, but most of it I learned another way. I did you a little bit of a favor."

Jacob squinted, waiting for it.

"I hired a private detective to see what she's been up to."

It took a moment for Jacob to process that. He wanted to be annoyed, but that would only make him a hypocrite especially since he'd done it just last year himself. "I guess you did do me a favor. I'm shocked you thought of it."

"What can I say? You're my best friend. Your shady ways have rubbed off on me."

"As if," Jacob chuckled. "What did you learn?"

"She's been looking for a job of course. She's had no luck. She just had a meeting with TCT for a show."

"You're kidding."

Ethan shook his head. "I'm not and I know you're close to some people over there."

Thompson Christian Television Network. Jacob had friends over there that were more like family. "Seems like the stars are lining up in my favor."

"You call it the stars. I call it God's favor."

"Yeah, I know, I get Christians shouldn't believe in luck, but some habits die hard. My mother believed the stars aligned."

"As long as you know what you believe," Ethan stated firmly. "Now, can we go pack your bags and get out of this place already? I'm not trying to get snowed in up here. I can't get a phone signal and I need to be amongst the living."

Jacob didn't move. He thought about Cameron. The

last time he'd talked to her he'd been so angry. It had been so long ago. Would she even be willing to speak to him now? Did he want to talk to her? Could they possibly make a relationship work after what she did? The pain in his heart wasn't quite as fresh as it had been years ago, but the way he felt about her when he wasn't thinking about the betrayal was.

*You're the love of my life. I'll never love another woman more,* he'd said. He shook his head. The words were like a curse he'd put on himself.

"You swore you'd try." Ethan's voice cut through his thoughts.

Jacob nodded. He hadn't just made that promise to Ethan. He'd made it to himself. He moved to the closet and reached in for the two suitcases he'd carried in the door when he'd arrived a month ago. He tossed one to Ethan. "You get the drawers and I'll get the stuff in the bathroom."

Ethan smiled, removed the hundred dollar bill from his pocket and tossed it onto the bed. "I told myself if you manned up I'd give you your money back."

Jacob guffawed and picked up the bill. "I may need it my friend. The idea that just popped into my head is going to require a lot of these." With that said, he went into the bathroom and began to pack.

# Chapter 3

"What makes you want to do reality T.V.?"

Jacob looked at the small group of programming execs that were assembled in the conference room of *Thompson Christian Television Network*. He gave special attention to the one in charge of new programming for the network Timothy Thompson, his undergraduate college roommate. Timothy, young like him, was open to more non-traditional shows for Thompson, especially when they were prepackaged and financed with O.P.M.- other people's money.

"I think the show could be a big success or I wouldn't be here," Jacob said. "I co-produced something similar in London and it did very well for two seasons.

Mason Thompson shook his head. "But the market here is saturated with these kinds of shows."

"The difference is the wholesome content. Your viewers aren't watching those shows because the values don't match theirs."

Timothy cleared his throat. "He's right, Mason. We've conducted some polls and found our viewers wanted to watch, but didn't like the secular values of the hosts. I think we've got something here."

"And the show won't be all talk. It's also not just about couples. Sure, we'll focus most of the show on relationships. Christian couples: newlyweds and couples getting back together and we'll include celebrities – I already have a few celebs and athletes on my short list of potential guests, but we'll also include everyday people on the show. People like your viewers who are working through issues."

Jacob was surprised by how excited he was about the show himself. This really did have potential. He continued, "We'll also do some features on people making second comebacks in business or ministry and we'll go to different locations, so it's not static. It's not just talk, talk, talk in the studio. It'll be…"

"Let's do it," John Thompson slammed a fist on the table. "I like it. I like it a lot."

Everyone in the room sat back. John, the head of TCTN had made a decision during a pitch meeting. He never did that. The room's occupants were visibly shocked. "I think it's time we stepped into this space." He stood, flipped his wrist and looked at his watch. "Jacob, it's been a pleasure to see you again. I look forward to working with you."

Relief washed over Jacob as he stood, walked around the table and shook the older man's hand.

"I've seen what you've been doing in Europe. I'm proud of you," John beamed at him. "I know you won't disappoint us." Followed by his secretary, he made a hasty exit.

Mason stood and reached for Jacob's hand. "I'm so surprised I hardly know what to say. He's been trying to stay clear of that kind of programming."

Timothy stepped up. "Grandfather can be a traditionalist, but even he recognizes changes and trends in the industry." He and Jacob pounded fists. "Welcome to TCTN."

Jacob let out long breath. He felt like he'd been holding it in the entire morning. "Thanks."

"Let's go back to my office and work through some details," Timothy said. They left the conference room and took a few short steps to the executive offices.

Jacob claimed one of the chairs across from Timothy's desk.

"I told you I just needed a meeting."

"That you did," Timothy replied, opening a cigar case on his desk and offering him one.

Jacob declined. "I think your grandfather has always liked me."

"My grandfather has watched everything you've done and raved about it." Timothy lit the cigar. He always thought you were smart and he knows a good deal when he sees one."

Jacob nodded. "When can we get started?"

Timothy's brow furrowed. "As soon as you want. The sneak preview episode for the pilot is brilliant. We like to do that. It helps build momentum. Do you have a celebrity couple in mind?"

"Kind of," Jacob replied. "I need to make some calls."

"Well, whoever you're thinking about is not as big as the person I have in mind. Let me confirm I can book them and I'll let you know."

Smiling, Jacob asked, "What, no hint?"

"Trust me, if it's a no you'll cry, so let me see what I can do and I'll get back to you."

Jacob agreed.

"In the meantime, hire your people. Let me know if you need to use our crew for the pilot. I'll set you up with publicity for a meeting tomorrow. They'll handle the website, social media and press stuff. We've got a studio that should work." Timothy paused. "You have anybody in mind for the host spot?"

"Yes, I already know who I want." Jacob hesitated for a moment like he was afraid to say her name. "Cameron Scott."

Timothy frowned. "Cameron Scott. She was the one from that *Saved Man* show right?"

"Yes and it was a pretty successful season for the show."

"The fiancé just dumped her."

"Yes."

"Is she working?"

"Not right now."

"Her reality television show career might be done. Any reason why you want to use her?"

"People love her. She's done this kind of forum before."

"Yeah, but she was no winner on that last show." Timothy took a few more puffs of his cigar, stubbed it out in the smokeless ashtray he was using, cut it and returned it to his cigar box. He raised an eyebrow and gave Jacob a knowing look. "You've got history with her."

Jacob allowed his lips to part in a smile. "Something like that."

Timothy shook his head. "It's not something that has the potential to go south is it?"

Jacob shook his head. "No. She needs the job. It'll be fine."

"I need this show to work. I've been trying to get these old folks to step into the new millennium for five years." Timothy chastened. "You're sure she's not going to be a distraction for you?"

Jacob thought about the deal he'd offered Thompson

which included his financing seventy percent of the production cost for the first three episodes of the season and then fifty percent for the last four. It was a lot of money, nearly most of what he had, but if the show was successful he'd earn it back. If he was successful as he hoped he'd be he would have Cameron too. "I'm never distracted when I have this much money on the line."

Timothy nodded. "I'm sure you're not." The seriousness of the moment was captured with a beat of silence, then he asked, "I'll assume you'll take care of contacting Cameron's agent?"

Jacob paused. "Actually, I'd like to leave my name out of the initial contact. Have one of your people call."

"Out of the blue?"

"You guys had her over here some weeks back for something. Just piggy back on that."

Timothy raised his chin and laughed. "You know more than I do. What's up with this woman?"

"She's just…don't make me tell you. Seriously, she needs the job and you can trust me, so I need you to do that."

Timothy laughed again. "All right man. I'll have someone from human resources get a package together."

"Great. If you can make it happen today that would be perfect. I don't want her to accept something else. She's been taking a lot of meetings."

"Consider it done." Timothy smiled. "But you do know you owe me the entire story."

Jacob grinned. "I'll tell it as soon as I get the ending I want."

Timothy shook his head. "The ending you want. Sounds like you need to be on the show."

Jacob laughed. "I've known her a long time. She has a strong work ethic. I also know she won't blow this opportunity."

"She did bring it on *Saved Man*. I've never seen a woman get a ring and so much media coverage afterward."

Cameron's face drifted into his mind. "It was that smile of hers. Not only is she gorgeous, she's also really sweet. People like that. I don't think she'll have trouble getting America to fall in love with her again."

"We'll hope for America, but I can tell she's had no problems hooking you." Timothy stood and Jacob followed. "Let's go get a studio and talk to our set designer."

They left the office. Timothy gave him a full tour. Thompson was a large operation by any studio's standards. Four floors with three full studios on each including storage space for equipment, meeting space and production rooms where all the decisions were made. Jacob was assigned a studio and office space on the second floor, and fortunately for his budget, the existing set had been for a talk show. Plans were made to refresh the paint and the artwork and bring in new seat cushions. Everything else could stay.

Jacob finished up at Thompson; picked up the car he leased from the parking lot and made the trip back to his hotel. He completed several phone calls on the way, the last being to the lawyer he'd hired to take care of Cameron. He had to make sure all his plans were set in motion. There could be no delays, because a delay could ruin everything.

# Chapter 4

Cameron was not in the mood for the subway and all that riding a public transportation system entailed. It was mainly the risk of being recognized and then having to deal with fans and not so fans that lurked and snapped pictures either way that bothered her most. She decided she wasn't going to make herself take it. She sank down in the seat of the taxi and closed her eyes. She needed to go home. It had been months since she'd seen her family. She was starting to think if she didn't get a job it might be where she had to go permanently.

Kirk, North Carolina, population six hundred eighty nosy, judgmental, people, was the last place she wanted to live. But maybe that's where she was supposed to be. Her mother needed her. Caring for her grandmother and a four year-old was hard. Her grandmother's care was a full-time job so her mother couldn't work outside the home. It was okay when Cameron had the money to pay for a home health aide to help, but she'd had to stop the service months ago.

Her grandmother's social security benefits were their only income and that was troublesome; troublesome because she collected just enough to make her ineligible for state medical assistance, barely enough to pay all the household expenses and definitely not enough to subsidize her medical care. All of those variables kept Cameron awake at night.

She felt the taxi come to an abrupt stop. Cameron opened her eyes and noted they were sitting in rush hour traffic. She let her gaze drop to the meter and noticed she was already at eighteen dollars. She reached into her bag and removed the twenty dollar bill she had there and called out to the driver to let her out. She shoved the money through the payment slot, pushed the door open and climbed out.

The freezing wind whipped across her face. Cameron shuddered. Walking the last four blocks home in the cold wouldn't kill her, even if her heels were nearly five inches high. Paying more than twenty dollars for a taxi was a definite no, no.

"I should have just taken the subway," she whispered to herself. "I'm walking anyway."

Cameron strode along taking note of all the little stores she'd never noticed before. She was one street over from her own, but the luxury of studio pickups, taxis, and driving, made her really unfamiliar with the surrounding neighborhood. After getting a few catcalls from some brothers parked on a stoop, Cameron pulled her handbag closer and picked up her pace. Manhattan. Million dollar apartments were literally down the street from abandoned dumps. The wealthy and homeless were in close proximity at all times.

Her phone made the low battery beep. Surprised that it was going dead already, she removed it and noticed she'd received a text message hours ago. It was a notification text advising her that the service was temporarily disconnected. She stopped and shouted at the phone angrily. "I was going to pay you as soon as I got home!" A turned off phone was the ultimate embarrassment. She'd been taught from her childhood that people never knew what went on behind your closed door, however if your phone was off all your business was in the street.

She returned the phone to her handbag and looked to the right. Cameron was standing outside of a liquor store. She stared at the items displayed in the window: Vodka, Gin, Rum, Tequila and wine. She recognized the brand names:

Absolut, Ciroc, Bacardi, Selvarey, Beefeater and Sutter Home. She felt the familiar pull. She began to perspire, even in the brisk cold.

*One drink*, she thought. She only wanted one, but she wanted that one really badly. One would relax her. Take all this stress away.

She hadn't drunk in years. What could one drink do? She began to twist the strap of her handbag. She was fighting with the leather. She was fighting with herself. She knew well what one drink could do, but still…she wanted it.

"Hey, you're Cameron Scott."

Cameron hadn't realized her eyes were still closed until she had to open them to see who was talking to her. It was a bike messenger. He'd stopped right in front of her.

"Can I have your autograph?" He reached into his pocket and pulled out what looked like a receipt and a pen.

Cameron swallowed, accepted the items and immediately flipped the "on" button all stars had inside of them and asked, "Who am I signing it to?"

"Kevin," he replied and he took out his camera and snapped a picture of her. "Can I get one with you?" he asked. "For Instagram."

Cameron nodded a yes and waited for him to get off his bike. They smiled and he took the selfie image. She handed him the paper. He let his eyes sweep her body from head to toe. "Your ex is a fool cause you sho"nuff finer in real life. Keep your head up." He climbed back on his bike and rolled away.

Cameron took a final look at the spirits in the window. *You're Cameron Scott*, he'd said. Those words had saved her. He'd reminded her who she was and that reminded her that she'd vowed to never take *one drink* again.

She entered her building and was glad to see the doorman hold up her Coach bag. "I've been guarding it with my very life."

"Ah, thank you so much," she said taking it from his hand. Getting her bag back was a little light in what had been a really dreary day.

"The sun will come out tomorrow, Ms. Scott," he said.

Cameron smiled. "If they made a black version of Annie, I'd audition."

"And you'd be great." He smiled back at her.

She took a few steps to the area where the mailboxes were housed and pushed the code for her box. Once it popped open, she removed the mail. There was one letter and based on the return address it was not going to be good. She opened it and read. Her hands shook so hard the letter slipped from her fingers and floated to the floor. She felt her heart constrict. Her breaths became painful and tight.

*Notice of Intent to Evict.*

She placed a hand against the wall to steady herself. "Oh my God." She looked to the left at the man who was also gathering his mail. "Oh my God." She wasn't sure if the words had come out of her mouth or if they were stuck in her head, but she didn't care. She was going to pass out. She had to breathe. She had mere seconds on her feet.

"Are you okay?" the man asked.

One second…

"I can get the doorman."

Two seconds…*BREATHE*

"Ma'am, are you having some kind of attack or something?"

Three…

"Are you Cameron Scott?" A voice came from the left of them. Cameron clutched her heart with her free hand and turned to the young man who'd entered the alcove. Tears had pooled in her eyes and clouded her vision. She could barely see him. Was it the marshal? Were they coming to put her out? She tried hard to suck in a breath, but her chest was too constricted. She rocked forward and backward and extended her hand to reach for her neighbor. She needed something to hold on to, but it was too late. Everything went black.

\*\*\*

Cameron stretched her legs out and took the cup of tea that her best friend, Stacy Young, offered her. She couldn't believe she'd actually fainted. She guessed a notice of eviction would do that to anybody, but she was more inclined to believe it was those meals she'd skipped over the past couple of days.

"Are you sure you don't need to go to the E.R? You never know about a head injury."

Cameron took a sip from the cup and winced from the pain of moving her head. "It's a bump. I don't have blurry vision or anything like that."

"But you have a headache."

"I have a tension headache, girl. I've had it all day. It has nothing to do with the fall."

"I'm so glad you didn't hurt yourself. People faint and break teeth when they fall the wrong way."

"God forbid," Cameron said. "It's a good thing I know to fall sideways."

Stacy grimaced. "Actresses. So much drama."

"I won't be acting when I put my things in the back of a truck later this week. That will be some reality for sure. Since you're here, I need you to help me start packing." Cameron raised a hand to her temple. The movement caused her head to hurt. "I already did my research. I have six days to get out." She took another sip of tea.

"I'd prefer to keep the faith and hold on a few more days. Maybe something will happen for you."

"Like the lottery?" Cameron smirked. "No chance of that. I don't play." She leaned forward, which caused more stabbing pain. "Maybe I'll pack tomorrow."

"I brought my bag. I'll stay here tonight so I can keep an eye on you."

She knew well why her friend was staying with her tonight. It wasn't that she didn't care about her. Stacy despised her roommate and was counting down the days until their lease was up. The two women had been friends since Cameron arrived in New York City, which had been three years ago. From their first meeting they'd been thick as thieves, each being the sister the other never had. "You and Leigh have another fight?"

"Her boyfriend is in town. You know what that means."

"Sex and weed?"

"For three days straight."

"Just stay here. There's no point in even going home until he's gone."

"I appreciate it," Stacy said. "I have early calls every morning this week and I need my sleep." Stacy was a self-employed personal assistant. She specialized in working with reality television stars and did things like keep their calendars, schedule events, take care of wardrobe requests and errands. She would even walk their dogs if they asked her. At any given time she provided services to three or four clients and it added up to really great money.

"Aren't you glad you're not working for me? One less demanding actor."

Stacy made a scoffing sound. "Please, you're my favorite client. I can't wait for you to get a job."

Cameron smiled. "How about working for free? Pass me that." She nodded toward the manila envelope the courier from the lobby had handed her when she'd come out of her fainting spell. "I'm sure that's got to be something about the eviction." She placed her mug on the sofa table behind her and accepted the envelope.

"The return address is for Thompson Television. Didn't you do a test or something over there?"

Cameron's jaw dropped. She quickly opened the envelope and began to read. "Dear Ms. Scott, we appreciate you testing for," she read to herself skipping the name of the show and getting to the point. *While we have decided on another candidate, we believe you would be perfect for the role as host for our new show, Second Chances…*" Cameron continued to read. When she was done she let the letter fall onto her lap. "Stacy, this is a job offer. They offered me a job hosting a show."

Stacy shrieked, picked up the letter and read. "It's testing with seven episodes."

Cameron closed her eyes and fought tears. She didn't know why she was fighting them so hard. They were finally happy ones. She opened her eyes and Stacy was smiling at her.

"That's enough of a run to get me out of debt. I can pay you back and find a new place to live."

Stacy collapsed on the back of the sofa. "I knew all that praying was going to pay off."

Cameron nodded, thinking about the many nights she lay on her face praying and crying and begging God for a job. She'd been optimistic that something would work out for her, until nothing had worked out for her.

"*Second Chances*," Stacy said, I wonder what it's about. It just says relationship talk. Is that going to be like what you were doing on *Heart*?"

Cameron shrugged and picked up her tea mug again. Suddenly her head felt better. "I can't imagine anyone would want me for that, but I don't care. It can't be but so crazy on Thompson. They don't compromise on programming."

Her phone rang and the face of her agent, Linda Sizemore, flashed on the screen. Taking a moment to pay her bill had been smart, because missing a call from Linda was not the business. She let her hand hover over the phone to answer it. Linda's voice came through the speaker, which was auto set to come on.

"I've been trying to reach you all afternoon. "You'll never guess who I talked to today!" she squealed with delight.

"Actually, I might be able to guess," Cameron replied picking the letter up. "Thompson Christian Television Network."

"How'd you know?"

"I received a letter by courier."

"Oh," Linda replied, "That's different. I wonder if I missed an email from them or something." Cameron could imagine the look on the woman's face. Thompson hadn't done the notification through her, which wasn't the way it was normally done, but Linda recovered quickly from the slight. "I'll call first thing in the morning and try to get you more money."

"The money is fine, Linda, please let's just take the

offer and find out when I need to show up."

"I need to negotiate something. Clothes, wigs, a big office. That's what you pay me for."

"You got me in the door which led to this offer, so please, just tell them I accept and leave it at that. I don't want anything to delay my contract." *Or my check*, she thought.

"Okay," Linda replied. "Did you find some place to live? If you need a loan until you get paid just let me know."

Her agent, much like a friend had been so generous to her, but she couldn't borrow any more money. She bit her bottom lip before speaking. "I worked it out. Thanks so much. Call me with the details as soon as you talk to them."

"Of course," Linda replied. "Get some sleep. You'll need your beauty rest."

Cameron ended the call.

"You've worked out your housing situation?" Stacy raised an eyebrow. "That must mean you're planning to sleep on my air mattress between eviction and the first check."

"I can't borrow any more money, so if the offer is still open."

"Of course it is. Did you find a storage place for your stuff?"

"No, I'll find something tomorrow."

"Are you sure you don't want to borrow some money to keep the landlord happy until you get paid?"

"I owe too much. I hate to be a slacker, but I can't catch that up. This offer is for seven thousand a week. After taxes, that'll hardly be four. No way I can pay seven in rent and save for the next rainy day."

"And send money home."

Cameron nodded. "Right and you know that I'd sleep in a box on the street to make sure that happens."

Stacy laid the letter from Thompson on the coffee table. "Well, there's no need to do that as long as I'm alive."

Cameron's heart smiled at Stacy's declaration. "What about Leigh? The last thing I need is a tabloid story about being homeless."

"Don't worry. She has no idea who you are. Remember, she doesn't watch T.V. She doesn't even own one." Stacy stood. "I'm going to make us some dinner." She walked into the kitchen.

"It's slim pickins in there. Ramen noodles or canned ravioli."

"In that case, I'll order take-out," Stacy yelled back.

Cameron closed her eyes and with all the spiritual energy she could muster, she thanked God from her soul. He'd thrown her a lifeline, an unbelievable save in the ninth hour. She just had to give the show her all and make it work. It wouldn't be easy, because the last topic she ever wanted to talk about was love.

# Chapter 5

The day had come. Cameron stepped through the entrance of the studio and heard her name being yelled from one of the upper floors.

"Cameron Scott!"

The midget of a woman, Cameron surmised her to be less than five feet tall, flew down a flight of steps. She approached holding her hand out for a shake, which Cameron gave. "Phyllis Dormer. I'm the runner."

Cameron smiled. Showrunner equaled her new boss of sorts. "Nice to meet you. I'm so excited—"

"I'm sure you weren't told, because you're late, that we have a staff meeting every morning at eight," Phyllis said, cutting her off. "I'd like you to be available for our production meetings at nine, well, Mr. Gray would and then you and I will meet at eleven a.m. We'll get into some pre-production filming after that."

Phyllis began walking and Cameron followed her.

"We'll talk show for a few days and then on Wednesday we'll film the first segment with Hunter Perry and his recycled fiancé. I can't remember her name."

Cameron stopped in her tracks. "Did you say Hunter Perry?"

"Yes," Phyllis smiled. "Mr. Thompson has been a mentor of his for years. I think that's why he agreed to the sneak peek episode. He knew he could get Hunter Perry on. I know it seems like we're on the fast track, but Mr. Perry is in town this week and what's convenient for him is convenient for us." They rode the elevator, walked a bit and Phyllis opened a door to a studio area. "This is the set. Watch the wet paint."

It was typical for shows of this nature, a stage with chairs and a small table and an arc of benches in front for the studio audience. It was a good size audience area, bigger than what they'd had on *Heart*.

"We're still working through some of the particulars. Mr. Gray is expecting us to come up with the actual flow of the show, so we'll film a hundred hours of Perry and his fiancé all so we can be sure to get anything we'll possibly need and then we can fold in the footage that works for the final concept." Phyllis was on the move again.

"Working backwards," Cameron said following. She was careful not to step on cable lines and various other fixtures on the floor.

"Working the way Mr. Gray wants us to," Phyllis replied. "But, yes, backwards."

Gray, Cameron thought. She thought Phyllis had said Gray the first time, but the woman's accent was coated with a heavy dose of Northern Jersey twang. All Cameron heard was meeting this and meeting that. She knew from experience that they had a lot of work to do and she'd be here long hours getting the show off the ground. From what Linda had shared with her, the show's seven episode test would air over the summer in seven of Thompson's markets including: New York, Atlanta, Charlotte, Richmond, Houston, Charleston and Jacksonville. It would air once a week. If received favorably, filming would continue for another five episodes and be placed in national syndication. But the early ratings had to be strong. The pilot or "sneak peek" episode was set to air in thirty days. It was a painfully short lead time.

"This way to your office," Phyllis said. They went down a long hallway. Phyllis provided a mini tour, announcing which room was for what purpose. Fortunately, they were all labeled so there would be no need for a map or breadcrumbs to find her way around. They finally came to a door that had Cameron's name on it. Phyllis opened it and walked through the small dressing room to another door that led into the actual office space. It was tiny, Cameron thought, but it was hers. It was a paycheck. Everything about this adventure with Thompson was a blessing. She didn't care if they did her makeup in the ladies room. She was glad to have a job.

"Your keys are inside the desk. Lock up your bag and join us in the production meeting room in ten minutes."

Cameron nodded. "Thank you."

"Don't thank me yet. I'm going to work you harder than you've ever worked." Phyllis didn't blink. "I'm not crazy about the lack of lead time and promotion for this show. It'll be an uphill battle to get sponsors, but I don't produce losers, so it's a challenge I'll rise to and so will my team."

Cameron put her bag on the desk. "Well, I can tell you no one wants it to be a success more than I do. I need this show."

Phyllis tilted her head and gave Cameron a once over with her eyes. "Good. I like hungry people. In my experience, desperation makes good clay, but I'm going to be honest with you. You would not have been my first choice for this based on what you did on *Heart*, so if I think you suck, I'm going to say so."

Cameron understood her situation all too well. Phyllis did not have to explain it to her. "That's fair," she replied.

Phyllis's eyes swept the room again. "Well, meditate or pray, whatever you do to get yourself going and I'll see you in nine minutes." She half turned toward the exit before adding, "You have an assistant. Stacy. She worked with you on *Saved Man* and *Heart*."

Pleased, Cameron nodded. "Yes, how did you know?"

"I do my homework," Phyllis said. Cameron thought the woman almost smiled. "I just talked to her. She'll be here this afternoon." Then Phyllis was gone.

Cameron whispered the words, "Thank you, Jesus." Excitement rushed through her veins. She walked around the desk and dropped into the plush leather chair. She reached into her bag for her phone. She had three texts from Stacy, but no sooner than she'd opened the first one she heard a light tap on the door. It opened and in walked... Jacob Gray. Her breath caught. Her heart stopped. Her phone hit the floor.

# Chapter 6

Jacob knew he'd shocked her, because her honey brown skin turned pale. While she recovered, he marveled at how beautiful she still was. Painful grimace across her face and all, she was gorgeous. He growled inwardly. Some women sucked the air out of a brother.

His mouth slid into an easy half grin and he kept his tone casual and even, like he'd spoken with her yesterday. "I didn't want you to walk into the production meeting without knowing."

Cameron squinted and shook her head like she was trying to shake his image away. "Mr. Gray. You're Salt Productions?" she asked referring to the production company listed on the contract she'd signed.

"I am," he replied stepping all the way into the room and closing the door behind him.

"But how?" she stuttered. "I thought you were in Europe."

"I was, but now I'm here."

"Why?"

"To produce this show."

Cameron made a sound, part snort, part moan. "I had no idea Salt Productions was your company."

"Then I've been keeping closer tabs on you than you've been keeping on me. Salt Productions Limited is the name of my London production company."

Cameron stood and cocked her head. "You're right. I haven't been keeping up with what you've been doing. Why would I?"

Jacob thought about mentioning the little detail that she had once vowed to be his life partner but he decided she might not like to hear that come out of his mouth. Not today anyway.

Cameron's hand went to her hip. "I don't believe in coincidences, so what are you up to?"

"I'm producing a television show."

"You don't do reality T.V."

"How would you know that if you weren't paying attention to what I was doing?" He stepped toward her.

She raised her free hand to stop him from moving. "You're good right where you're standing." She rolled her eyes. "And the answer is I know all the reality T.V. shows because I've been looking for work."

"In London?" he chuckled. "Maybe you have been keeping closer tabs on me than you're willing to admit."

She gave her head a wry shake. "Don't you believe that."

Jacob cleared his throat. He'd made his mind up last night that he'd be honest with her. "I hired you because you needed a job. I heard about what happened with *Heart* and then how that jerk, Housely, dumped you. Word on the street is you need work. I thought I could help you."

"Word on the street." Cameron crossed her arms over her chest. "You're kidding right?"

"I'm here."

"Gray, I haven't talked to you in five years. You divorced me last year, so why in the world would you come back to the U.S. to produce a show for me?"

Despite the icy look in her eyes, Jacob took a step in her direction. "Because I care about you. You've been out of work and I thought I could help."

She emitted a sound like laughter, but its tone had no humor. "I can't believe you just gave me that answer. A pity job."

"I don't pity you. You're talented. You just needed a break."

"Then why not ask one of your buddies in the industry to give me one? Why come back?"

Jacob frowned. "It was time for me to come home. I've been gone long enough, besides this part of the world doesn't belong to you."

She dropped her hands from her chest. They settled on her hips. "It's been nice having you out of it."

He gave her a hard glare. He would have replied to her barb, but the placement of her hands on her hips had a brother distracted. God, she was beautiful.

"And, for the record," she said snatching him out of his fantasy. "I could have found my own job. You're out of your element. The last thing I need is another flop. I really will be done."

"It won't flop. I hired one of the best runners in the business and we're well funded."

Cameron didn't say anything at first. She seemed to be mulling over what he said. "I hope you're right about Phyllis."

"I am," he declared. "Plus who doesn't love a come back show? We've all wanted a second chance at something, haven't we?"

Cameron reached for a legal pad and pulled a pen from her handbag. "I need to get to my meeting."

He opened the door and swept a hand through the open space. "We need to, but after you."

She hesitated for a moment. The office was tiny and he wasn't planning to move to make passing him any easier. She dropped her handbag in the desk drawer and turned the key. Then after hesitating again for a moment she walked toward the door, toward him. He reached for her hand as she passed. Cameron snatched it back with so much force she hit the doorjamb and winced from the pain.

"I'm sorry about that. I just wanted to say, it's really good to see you, Cam. It's been a long time and I …I'm glad you're well. I'm –" It was he who was hesitating now. What did he think he was doing? Blabbing everything about how he felt out in the first meeting? If looks could kill he'd be dead from the venomous glare she was giving him. "I'm sorry. I shouldn't have touched you."

Cameron sighed. The look in her eyes shifted from annoyance to hurt. "I need this job, Gray. Please don't do anything to make me regret I took it."

She'd called him Gray and it warmed his heart. She was the only person on the earth that called him that and he'd missed it. "I won't," he replied, but he was talking to her back. She'd already passed through the dressing room and walked out the other door.

# Chapter 7

Cameron was late. It was only two minutes, but Phyllis chastised her with her eyes. She didn't say anything presumably because she'd walked in with Jacob Gray on her heels.

"I see you've met Cameron," Phyllis said to him.

"Cameron and I know each other, *well*," Jacob replied taking a seat next to her.

*Well*, she thought. He was starting already. She so hoped he'd do the right thing and sit across the conference room, but that would have been out of character for him. He'd never been a fan of doing something just because it was the right thing to do. She gave him the side eye, but then affixed a smile to her face because the entire staff was watching her.

"Everyone, this is Cameron Scott, our host. Cameron, this is the production team." Phyllis said and she proceeded to introduce everyone on the team to her. They had name tents in from of them and a young woman Phyllis introduced as her assistant popped up and put a tent in front of Cameron. Phyllis rolled her eyes like she thought that had been a silly thing to do. The woman got wind of her folly and held the other tent, presumably for Gray against her chest as she took a seat.

"Thank you, Ann, but I'm sure everyone knows who Cameron and Mr. Gray are."

"Jacob." His strong, smooth, baritone voice rang out in the room and Cameron's heart skipped a beat. His masculine timbre radiated in her ears. The heat from his body warmed his cologne and infused the air with it. Both were equally distracting and more familiar than she cared to think about.

Why oh why did he have to come back looking so durn good? Why wasn't he fat or ugly? She knew he was only thirty, but couldn't he be bald and toothless? And why for the love of God did that indigo blue suit cling to him like that?

She didn't even need to ask that question. She already knew the answer, because the brother spent time in the gym, working it out and keeping all that Jacob Gray fineness on point. She sighed. He hadn't changed a bit and that was not going to be easy to be around every day.

"What do you think, Cameron?" she heard Phyllis' voice pull her from her thoughts.

Thoughts of Jacob were set aside. She'd messed up. On her first day. At her first meeting, she wasn't listening. She opened her mouth but before she could speak she felt Gray's hand on hers. "That's not a pressing item, so let's give Cameron a little time to mull that over and come back to it in the morning."

She looked down at his hand on hers and then up at him. His honey colored eyes bore into hers. They hadn't changed either, but of course she hadn't expected them to. Those dreamy irises were a gift from God and no matter how old or fat or bald he ever became they'd capture the attention of anyone looking into them. She dropped her eyes to their intertwined fingers.

Gray smiled a little and to her dismay it also felt familiar and reassuring. Those were the last things she wanted to think about her ex-husband. She snatched her hand free and turned her chair so her back was facing him, but even then she could feel the heat of his eyes on the back of her head.

She jotted her thoughts on the legal pad and pushed it

in front of him.

**Stop staring at the back of my head.**

Gray reached for the pen, his hand brushed hers and once again a wave of heat rushed through her. He wrote, **You don't have eyes in the back of your head, so you don't know what I'm doing. Wishful thinking?**

She turned a bit and cast him a warning look. "Don't count on that," she whispered.

"Cameron, did you have something you wanted to share?" Phyllis asked.

Gray stood. "I think I'm a distraction, so I'll go. Cam, let's have lunch and catch up." He put a hand on her shoulder, squeezed and left the room. There were ten people in the room and ten sets of eyeballs on her. She picked up her pen like she was poised to take some notes and nodded for Phyllis to continue. Phyllis picked up where she left off as if she'd never stopped. Cameron tried to concentrate on the discussion in the room, but her shoulder seemed to be on fire in the spot where Gray had squeezed. How dare he keep touching her?

She'd have lunch with him, because first and foremost she was going to straighten him out on how this working together thing was going to flow. Secondly, she wanted to find out why in the devil he thought he had a right to waltz back into her life.

# Chapter 8

Gray had asked her to meet him at a Thai restaurant across the street from the studio. She knew he didn't care for Asian food of any kind, but Thai was her favorite and she'd heard this particular restaurant was one of the best in the city. If he was hoping for some grace, she wasn't extending any just because he'd picked a hot spot to eat. But even as that thought entered her mind she wasn't sure where she was going with it. Grace for what? What did she think he wanted? She didn't have anything. He was doing her a favor. The question that had been reverberating in her head all morning was why?

The aromas of garlic, curry, and fresh herbs filled the air and caused her stomach to knock. Jacob was already seated when she entered. Phyllis was across from him. When she approached the table, Phyllis popped up and said, "I promised I only needed five minutes and I had them." She turned toward Cameron and said, "Enjoy your lunch." Cameron doubted if that would happen. She nodded and watched the woman go to the cashier stand and pick up a bag, which she presumed was take-out, then she left.

"She's a piece of work." Cameron slid into the seat across from him. "I can already tell you have the right runner."

Gray's expression was unreadable, but if she had to assign a word for it she'd say he looked annoyed. "She doesn't think I have the right host."

Cameron could hear the disappointment in his voice. "Was she just talking about me?"

He didn't answer the question. "You'll prove her wrong." He raised a hand to signal the waiter that we were ready and the man popped right over to the table. "I'll have the Stuffed Wings and can I assume you'll have your favorite, the Basil Chicken?"

She swallowed before replying and glanced down at the menu for a moment to choose something other than her favorite food in the entire world. "I'll have the Avocado and Shrimp salad. Hold the curry, please."

The waiter took the menus and walked away.

Gray raised an eyebrow. "I'm surprised. I guess some things have changed."

She reached for her water goblet. "I still love it, but I'm working. I don't want to smell like garlic all afternoon." She took a long sip and placed the glass on the table. "Why does Phyllis think I'm wrong?"

He shrugged. "I don't know. She says it's her gut."

"She's had a lot of hit shows."

"She's had some failures too."

"Well, she knows what she's doing."

Jacob snatched his head back. "That doesn't sound like the Cam I know. You never lacked confidence like that. Where's the woman who walked into Film 101 and said she was going to produce an Emmy, Oscar and Tony winning production before she turned forty?"

Cameron swallowed. She'd completely forgotten about that ridiculous declaration. "First off, please, don't call me Cam."

"You called me Gray."

"If you ask me not to, I won't." Their eyes locked for a moment and then he smiled. She continued. "Secondly, don't even try to take the position that you know me, because you don't. We haven't seen each other in five years and if I remember it correctly, we had a fight that would knock the confidence out of any woman. Not that I allowed you to do that to me, but I'm sayin' you don't know me anymore. You don't know where I've been, what I've had to do, who I am or what I want to eat."

He was quiet for a moment. The expression on his face conveyed reflection. "You are absolutely right. It has been five years."

"And on that note, please tell me the truth about why you're here? Why are you doing this show? Why did you hire me?"

"Cam-eron," he said adding the second syllable to her name. "I told you already. It was time. I have some friends at Thompson, so I decided to approach them to do a show."

"But you don't do reality T.V."

"And I've never seen you order anything that didn't have basil in it at a Thai Restaurant, but you just did it." He paused. "People change."

"Well, I know that," she spat with all the venom she could manage, "but going from doing documentaries about athletes and sports to second chances..." She stopped. Her mouth dropped open and froze there. "*Second Chances*. Why on earth would you choose a topic like that?"

Gray's eyes had already been boring into hers, but now they took on an even more serious look. "Because." He paused for a long moment. "Maybe I want a second chance, Cam. Maybe I want that chance with you."

# Chapter 9

Jacob waited for Cameron to close her mouth. It took her a full minute to pick her chin up off the floor. He hadn't intended to come out and say it that way, but he'd always been a straight shooter. When his mind was made up, he went for it. His mind was made up about her. He wanted to try again or at least he wanted to talk about it.

Cameron stood and picked up her handbag. "I can't believe you would do this." She shook her head and leaned across the table. Once their faces were inches from each other she hissed, "I'm about as interested in you as I am in the flu." She stood upright and flew out of the restaurant.

"Okay, so that didn't go well," he said to himself, but it was to be expected. A lot of time had passed and she was bitter about it. She had some nerve. She was the reason they'd broken up in the first place. She had cheated on him, not the other way around. He expected her to be shocked that he wanted them to try again, but not because she considered him a virus. Shocked because he'd forgiven her and was ready to move forward. Sure, it took him some time to get to this place, but he'd arrived. The least she could do was appreciate it. *Women.* Did they always have to be so predictably difficult?

Jacob called the waiter over to his table, asked him to wrap up the meals and bring the check. After receiving his bag, he returned to the studio. He went straight to Cameron's office and knocked. When she didn't invite him in, he called, "Cameron, I know you're in there. Let me at least bring your food in?"

Her voice sounded from behind his. "I'm here." She sounded pitifully weak, but she looked even worse. Her eyes were wet with the residue of tears. He used his free hand to open the door and she walked in past him. "I'm not hungry."

"I don't eat avocados."

"Give it to someone else."

"I brought it for you."

"Just like you brought this studio space and this show. All so you could come back here and tell me you want a second chance. You think you can impress me by spending money?" A tension filled moment passed, then Cameron said, "I'm not as naïve as I used to be. I'm not impressed with your money. You can't buy me."

Jacob closed the door. "I'm not trying to buy you. I really wanted to help you get back on your feet."

"But there are strings attached."

Jacob shook his head. "I'm not strong arming you into anything."

"Good, because they have a name for that in the workplace. It's called sexual harassment."

He held his head at an inquisitive angle. "Can we just sit here and eat? I'll ask you some questions and you ask me some. It's called catching up."

Cameron shook her head. "I don't think there's a point. I'm not interested in knowing what you've been doing. I don't want to catch up on anything but my bills."

He studied her for a moment and then asked, "Where's your daughter?"

Cameron's head swirled to the right. She looked confused for a moment. "What did you just ask me?"

He cleared his throat, hesitating because her body

language wasn't lost on him. "I asked where your daughter was? Is she here in New York?"

Cameron stood and crossed her arms. "If you don't have anything to say about the show, I'd really like you to leave."

He swallowed. "I'm sorry. I just wanted to…"

"Get caught up. You said that already, but like I said, I'm not interested."

He stood. Removed her salad and utensils from the takeout bag and placed them on the desk and turned to leave.

"Gray."

He made an about face spin when he heard her voice.

"How did you know I had a daughter?"

He shrugged. "You haven't heard from me in five years, but that doesn't mean I haven't been keeping up with you." He turned the doorknob and left the office.

# Chapter 10

Cameron breathed a sigh of relief when she approached her apartment door and there wasn't a final writ of eviction taped to it. It had been four days. She was packing all day tomorrow and the movers were coming early the next day to take her things to storage. Sleeping on Stacy's floor was not a good option when she had to get up and be fresh for the show every day, so Stacy had loaned her some money and gotten a friend of hers to book her a super discounted room at the Millennium Hotel. Her plan was to stay there until she received her first paycheck from the show. Then she could look for another place to live.

Cameron turned the key in the lock. Before she could get inside she heard her name. It was the building manager. She swallowed, turned fifty shades of red and faced him. Eviction was so embarrassing.

He stopped a few inches closer than she would have liked and asked, "I was wondering if you needed anything?"

Cameron was thinking *uh yeah, a few more weeks*, but replied, "Needed anything like what?"

"The concierge put out a list of the new services that were available and I didn't see that you'd signed up for anything."

Cameron shook her head. "I don't understand. What services would I sign up for? I'll be moving in a few days."

"Moving?" The man looked confused. "Where are you going?"

"I'm being evicted. Surely you know that."

"Ms. Scott, you're not being evicted." His tone was not sarcastic or teasing. There was no humor in it at all.

"I received the notice of eviction."

"It must have crossed in the mail. Your rent was paid a week ago. We have the full balance, so there is no eviction pending."

Cameron's heart began to pound. It was pounding so hard it felt like it was going to come out of her chest. This was the second time that had happened to her today. The first was upon seeing Gray and now... "I, I hadn't heard from my accountant. I didn't know that the entire balance was caught up."

"Yes, it most certainly is. In fact, I believe you're current for next month as well." He paused for a moment. "I'll have the concierge send a list of the services up and stick it under the door for your review. The housekeeping in particular is very reasonable and the company is bonded."

Cameron nodded. "Thank you." She pushed the door, walked in and then fell back against it.

Hot tears forced their way out from under her closed eyelids. The entire amount was paid in full. She didn't have to rush to move. How in the world...and then she realized...Gray. He'd saved her again.

She removed her coat, walked into her bedroom and stretched out on the bed. She was home now, so she allowed herself to think about him. Those eyes she'd been trying hard not to let wander through her mind were there now, staring into her soul. Jacob Gray was back in her life, first the show and now the apartment.

She found it interesting that he'd done that. He'd paid her rent for an entire year when he left her the first time. Then it had only been seven hundred dollars a month and although she was glad she didn't have to pack her things and move back home to Kirk in disgrace, the obligatory gesture on his part was no match for the heartache she'd encountered when he was gone. He'd disappeared without a trace. Not even his father knew where he was for two years or at least that's what she'd been told. And now he was back without warning and she couldn't help but resent him for the intrusion. Yes, she'd prayed and prayed for a lifeline, but why did God have to use the one person who hurt her most to be the one who saved her?

Her phone rang the tone she'd set for her mother.

"I was just about to call you," she said sitting up. "How are you?"

"I'm fine. How's the new job, baby?"

Cameron's shoulder's dropped. She pushed her back into the pillows. "I had a good first day."

"Is the producer nice?"

Cameron shook her head. "This is New York, Mama. Nice is relative. I can work with her. Everyone seems nicer than the other shows I've been on. Maybe because it's Christian."

"Well then that's a blessing?"

"Where's Charity?" Cameron's four year old's face came to her mind. Her heart rate sped up in anticipation of hearing her voice.

"She's in bed. You know she goes to sleep at seven."

Disappointed, Cameron nodded like her mother could see her. "Let her Skype me in the morning before she leaves for school."

Her mother paused. "I can't do that, baby. Our internet and stuff is off. We couldn't pay the bill."

Cameron's head dropped. "Mama, why didn't you

tell…" she paused. Her mother didn't have to tell her. Cameron knew. Her mother was trying not to be a burden. "I'm so sorry. I get paid on Monday. I promise I'll send money right away."

"Internet and cable don't mean nothing to us. You know we don't care about that stuff. You pay your rent before they evict you."

Cameron hesitated. She wanted to tell her mother her good news, but she didn't want a bunch of questions or a lecture about Jacob Gray. "I worked something out. I'll get you money as soon as they give me my check." She cringed before asking the next question. "Do you have food?"

"Baby, please don't worry about us."

"Mama, I have to ask."

"Yes, we have food. I did a little sewing last week. I made dresses for a set of sextuplets over in Asheville. Can you believe six babies at once?"

Relief rushed through her. She responded to her mother. "Sounds like a litter."

"A blessing," her mother said. "Children are always a blessing."

Cameron was silent again. She didn't miss her mother's emphasis on the word *always*. Like she didn't know that.

"What color were the dresses?"

"Pink and blue and lavender. I'm still making them. They ordered three sets. The grandmother is wealthy. It must be nice to be rich and able to do whatever you want for your grandchildren. Nice for the children too."

Cameron swallowed. She knew where her mother was going with this. It was her belief that Charity could benefit from her paternal grandfather's money. Her mother had hinted at it many times, but sharing Charity with that family was out of the question. God himself was going to have to tell her she had to do that.

"What are the dresses for?" Cameron asked moving the conversation along.

"Church. I guess they're Christian people. Anyway, I finished one set and she paid me. It was enough to buy food and your grandmother's diapers."

Cameron nodded. Guilt filled every pore in her body. She could jump off a bridge with a noose around her neck for what she'd done. She'd messed up on *I Heart*. If she'd just done the show the right way, her family wouldn't have suffered. She wouldn't have durn near gotten evicted. But she hadn't done right. She'd gotten a big head. She had thought more of herself than she should have and messed up that job. "After this set of dresses you tell her you can't do anymore. I'll be sending money again."

"Cameron, one thing I learned in life is to never put all your eggs in one basket. Now your grandmother is a little better than she was, so I'm going to take in work as much as I can to keep a nest egg saved up."

Her mother was talking sense. The good sense she'd taught her, so she wasn't going to rebut that. "I hear you. I'm going to do the same."

"I've got to go. I try to work on a dress in the evenings when everybody is asleep. You get some rest."

Cameron looked at the clock on the wall across from her. It was only eight p.m. "I will. I'm going to call Charity before she leaves for school."

"Okay, I'll make sure she waits for you."

Cameron smiled and whispered. "Thank you, Mama."

"You don't have to thank me for anything," her mother replied. "I love you, baby."

They ended the call.

Cameron closed her eyes tight. *Children are always a blessing.* Charity was a blessing. The only reason she wasn't here with her was because of her work schedule. Her mother wouldn't accept that. Her mother didn't accept her decision to be in New York at all. Cameron wasn't sure what her mother expected her to do with a degree in mass communications in Kirk, North Carolina. Check groceries at the Save-a-Lot Supermarket? That would not have paid their bills.

The decision to come to New York was the right one and she had no regrets, not even having to leave her sweet little girl behind. But now it had been almost four months since she'd been home. She was no long distance driver. Six hours was about her max. When money got tight, she couldn't afford the plane fare. That was all changing thanks to… she shook her head. *Thanks to Gray.*

Her schedule for the next month was demanding. She was working almost six days a week, but she'd get home again as soon as she could. She picked up her phone and called Stacy to report the good news about not having to move.

Cameron was glad they hadn't assigned some random intern to work with her. Stacy was a top notch assistant. She anticipated Cameron's every need before Cameron knew it herself.

"Explain. What happened?" Stacy asked.

Cameron told her the production company paid her rent. She felt guilty, but it was only a little white lie. She wasn't in the mood for the fanciful romance that Stacy would make out of Gray paying it.

"The production company is your ex-husband."

"No, it's his production company and I guess they

didn't want the bad publicity of me being put out on the street by the marshal."

"Puleeze. He makes all the decisions. I can't believe he paid all your back rent."

Cameron couldn't believe it either. It was so much money, but it was nothing compared to what the show was costing him. She was sure most of it had to be Gray's money, because that's how these things worked. He had to be in for over a quarter of a million, possibly double that depending on the terms he'd negotiated. She didn't know how to take that; him risking a fortune on a show for her, so she sidestepped it.

"I guess he's still rich, huh?"

*Not after this investment*, Cameron thought. "He had some successful projects."

"How do I love him? Let me count the ways…let's see, he made a show so you would have a job. He paid durn near twenty thousand in back rent. He couldn't get any more handsome. What else does he have to do?"

"Do? What do you mean?"

"I mean what else does he have to do to prove he's still in love with you?"

Cameron wasn't about to tell Stacy that Gray had already admitted how he felt about her. She hadn't processed it herself, so she feigned indifference. "Stacy, you're a cracked pot."

"No, I'm not. That man has spent a small fortune on you. Pretty soon you're going to have to make a decision."

"About what?"

"About how you feel about him."

"I already know how I feel about him." Cameron rolled her eyes. "Let's change the subject." They talked a few more minutes and then Cameron ended the call and went into her bathroom. She didn't really need to use it, but she had to change her position. Nervous energy was erupting from her pores. She ran her fingers through her hair and tried to stop her emotions from taking over her thoughts. She stared at her reflection in the mirror. Her face was still made up from her day on the set. She was well put together from the top of her head to the shoes on her feet, but her eyes were telling. Gray's return to her life had her on edge.

*"I'd like us to try again."*

Cameron closed her eyelids tight. When she opened them, uncertainty stared back at her from the vanity mirror. The show had been the best news she'd received in forever. She wasn't going to be homeless. Though it was nearly impossible to feel peace about it. Jacob Gray had spent a lot of money. Now she owed him. Like all bills, this debt would come due. One day she'd have to pay him back. Cameron just hoped she wouldn't pay with her heart.

# Chapter 11

Her life was back on track. Cameron stepped onto the stage of the Winnie Walker show and waved to the studio audience. This show was the last thing she expected to do today, but Thompson's publicity department had been trying to get her on and Winnie had a cancellation.

Winnie Walker was a premiere media personality and author. She hosted a syndicated daytime television talk show, The Winnie Walker Show. Everyone who was anyone wanted some airtime on it. Winnie was typical of celebrity gossips…celebrating with you like a bestie when things were good and talking about you like an enemy when things were not.

Another round of applause came from the audience as Winnie took Cameron's hands in hers. They air kissed. Cameron had grown up with the real hugs and kisses you exchanged in the south, but she'd gotten used to the New York way and found she liked it. She didn't have to worry about allowing a two-faced snake like Winnie to get that close.

They sat down in their respective chairs under the continued applause of the studio audience. Cameron looked out at Winnie's crowd and smiled. She remembered the last time she'd been on the show. She'd been with Rick right after *Saved Man* had ended. They were a newly engaged couple and she was showing off that monstrous ring he'd given her. The next time she heard Winnie speak her name it was to poke fun at her for the broken engagement. Winnie was great at her job as a celebrity gossip commentator. She covered all the highlights and low moments as expected, but she did it obnoxiously well.

At the instruction of a stagehand, the audience began to quiet the roar of their applause.

"So, Cammmeron." Winnie sang her name, paused briefly and looked at her from head to toe. "It's good to see you again."

Cameron worked hard to keep the smile on her face. "It's great to be back."

"You look fantastic, diva."

"Thank you. So do you."

"I've always admired your taste in clothes." Winnie reached across the space between them and touched the hem of her skirt. "Is that a Prabal Gurung?"

"I think so."

"It is. I know Prabal Gurung because I can't fit anything he designs. He makes the best prints, but his sizing is for skinny women."

The audience was prompted to laugh and they did so.

Cameron laughed with them. "Winnie, you look great. You can fit a Gurung."

"I can, but it'll be tight. I'm telling you he doesn't make anything for Amazons like me." She paused. "And speaking of weight. You weigh a little less. The last time I saw you had a five pound ring on your finger." Winnie reached for the coffee mug closest to her and took a sip of water. Cameron wanted to take her mug and throw the contents in Winnie's face.

"I did indeed and it feels great to have gotten rid of that dead weight," she retorted.

"Touché' Diva, touché. That Rick Housely was fine,

but honestly I think there's something funny about him."

Cameron grimaced. "Rick's a great guy. I mean we aren't going the distance for our reasons, but he'll make someone a nice husband one day."

Winnie grimaced and shook her head. "No he won't. There's something off…"

Cameron frowned. "What do you mean off?"

"I'm going to be honest, because you know that's all I can do." Winnie leaned forward like she was telling Cameron a secret. Like the mic wasn't on and no one would hear. "He makes my gaydar go off."

On cue the audience gasped.

"Am I the only one?" Winnie asked. She stood and pointed out to the audience. "Tell me, does he make your gaydar go off, ladies?" Some of the women applauded. Dramatic effect completed, Winnie took her seat again. "I guess we'll find out down the road, because they can never hide it forever," she said. "So, Cameron, let's talk about the new show. Tell us about *Second Chances*."

Cameron was glad the conversation shifted. The new show was something easy to talk about.

Winnie listened attentively. Cameron looked at the large clock off stage and knew that she had ninety seconds left on the stage with Winnie before her segment was done. She wondered if Winnie could embarrass her again in that short amount of time.

"Look, so your entire career on television has been about dating and relationships, *Saved Man*, then *I Heart* and now *Second Chances*. What's going on with your love life? Are you dating? Anybody hot we need to know about?"

Cameron threw up her hands. "Not right now. I'm focusing on my career."

"Hogwash, honey. That Housely did you dirty. The best way to get back at him is to find you a new man."

The audience was cued to applaud loudly in agreement.

Cameron tried to laugh. It was obvious that Winnie could find a way to embarrass her no matter how little time she had to work with. Cameron struggled to unclench her teeth, but her words came out tighter than she'd meant for them to. "I think from here on out I want to keep my love life private."

"Impossible. You're a reality T.V. star. You can't be private. You can't go back. And you're such a gorgeous creature. We need to get you set up on date."

Cameron teasingly leaned forward, in her head she counted down the seconds until the break. "Do you know somebody?"

"I don't. I don't know anybody who's fun enough for you. Because you were fun on the show, but I have an idea." Winnie reached for her phone.

*Was she calling a man?* Cameron thought. She looked at the clock. Twenty seconds. Winnie couldn't make a phone call in that time.

"I have over two million people following me on Twitter. Surely someone knows somebody they can hook you up with, so I just tweeted…Help Me Find a Date for Cameron Scott."

The audience was cued to applaud. Cameron was mortified, but she smiled just as the clock stopped.

# Chapter 12

"I can't stand that woman." Cameron roared as she slung her bag into the chair on the opposite side of her dressing room. Seconds later, Mary Sloan entered the room with Phyllis behind her. Mary was the head of publicity for Thompson Television. She was a tall sharp woman about twice Cameron's age with shocking white hair that added to the elegance her graceful height already gave her. Phyllis and she were an odd couple, but lately they'd been glued at the hips. Mary was personally handling the publicity for *Second Chances*, especially since they had Hunter Perry. Her reputation as a media pit bull was the reason Thompson was so successful. Her motto was "It didn't matter how great a show was, if no one knew it existed, it was a dud." She actually had that engraved on a sign outside her office door.

"It was good publicity for the show and you. Did you know you were trending? You haven't trended since you and Rick got engaged." Mary extended her iPad.

"I appreciate you being kind, but the last time I trended was when Rick broke up with me." Cameron reached for the iPad. "My cell phone battery is dead, so I couldn't check in the car." The rest of her thought died on her lips. She couldn't believe her eyes. Winnie and her followers were trying to pair her with every single man in the United States. They were posting pictures and bios and telephone numbers. This was insane.

"Well, I had an idea. I need to run it by management, but I think we should capitalize on this. We should have a charity event. Men donate and the prize is they get date with you," Mary said.

Cameron nearly choked on the sip of water she'd taken from the bottle Stacy handed her. "Are you kidding?"

"No. You're young, gorgeous and single. You're doing a show about folks in love, so I think it can only push ratings to have some side thingy going."

Cameron frowned. This idea was more ridiculous than Winnie's stupid tweet. "Men are not going to pay to go on a date with me. I'm not Kim Kardashian."

"You don't have to be. You're popular, more popular than you think. And you're gorgeous. Men like that. We'll reach out to some single athletes. Jacob knows a lot of them. We'll ask them to start the donating. Other men will follow suit." Mary made the statement like it was done already. That's how confident she was.

Cameron shook her head. "I don't like this."

"This is the business, Cameron. You know we have to work side angles and garner publicity wherever we can. I think Winnie did us a favor," Phyllis said.

Cameron sucked it up. She was not going to argue with either one of them. She thought it was dumb idea, but they were in charge.

"I'm going to go talk to management about it and get my people on it." Mary left the room and Phyllis followed.

Management was Gray. Cameron decided she didn't have anything to worry about. He wouldn't go for it.

She retrieved her purse, plugged her phone in and booted it up. Her Twitter page was the first stop. She gasped when she saw the number of tweets from men saying, "Hey, Cameron, I'll go on a date with you."

Stacy smiled. "Cheer up. You're likely to get an awesome wardrobe out this."

Cameron gave Stacy a weak smile. "Do you ever think

about anything but clothes and men?"

Stacy grimaced and pulled her phone from her pocket. She scrolled for a few moments and handed the phone to Cameron. "Did you see that?"

Cameron looked at a picture of Rick Housely. He'd just tweeted a nasty post about Winnie Walker. Then behind it stated he wished Cameron the best with finding love.

Cameron sighed. The entire world was in her business and if she knew him like she thought she did, that would not be Rick Housely's last tweet.

\*\*\*

This had been the longest day ever. Cameron stepped into the corridor and nearly jumped through the ceiling when she saw Gray standing there. "You scared me."

He reached for the tote bag she carried. "You're here late."

"I had some things I needed to take care of before we tape in the morning."

He nodded. "So, it looks like a lucky man is going to win a date with you."

"I'm surprised you okayed it."

Gray drew a long deep breath. "I couldn't think of a reason to say no." He paused a beat and then said, "Well, not one that I could say publicly."

"This is embarrassing you know. Just because Rick dumped me doesn't mean I need America to find me a date."

"I know that, but it'll be harmless. I hope." He paused like he wanted to add something. "The good news is people are talking about you with excitement and that's what matters. Your website has had twenty thousand hits today and with the show being on the home page its good stuff."

Cameron let out a long breath and pulled her handbag to her shoulder. They fell in step with each other, walking without speaking. The gesture felt oddly intimate to her, so she broke the silence. "What charity?"

"Ethan Wright's Youth Fitness Foundation."

She nodded. "Good choice."

"And we've decided to do it as a raffle."

Cameron stopped walking. "A raffle? Are you kidding? I could end up having dinner with a psycho." The elevator door opened. They stepped inside.

"No. The tickets range between fifty dollars and a thousand and you get a point for each fifty dollar increment of the ticket."

"Psychos have fifty dollars."

Jacob chuckled lightly. "Yeah, I supposed they do."

Cameron didn't appreciate him laughing about it. She was the one with all the risk. "What if nobody buys tickets?"

Jacob shook his head. "Nobody buy tickets?" His gaze caught hers. He let his eyes sweep her body from head to toe. "Men will be standing in line to buy tickets."

Cameron felt the blood pumping through her veins faster. Gray could say a lot with his eyes and what he'd just said was salacious.

"Don't worry about it," he said. "Mary and her team will do a great job. They're actually excited about it."

Cameron resigned herself to being stuck. "When will I get the details?"

"As soon as Mary and I work them out."

They stepped outside of the elevator and exited the building. The temperature had risen a bit over the past couple of days, so it was not as cold or wet as it usually was.

Jacob was walking closer to her. In fact, he was so close that Cameron could feel the heat from his body and smell the faint scent of his waning cologne. He stopped when they reached the curb. His eyes burrowed into hers so deeply she had to look away. "I have a car. Let me take you home."

Heart pounding, she could barely open her mouth. "A taxi will be fine."

"You should have a car."

"Gray, you've already spent enough money on me. I…" she paused. "I really appreciate you paying my rent."

The corner of his mouth turned up. "I couldn't have you on the street."

"It was a lot of money."

"A cost of doing business," he replied. "Celebrity evictions always make the headlines."

"Of course," she replied, feeling silly that she'd gotten the wrong impression about his reasons. "We wouldn't want me to attract more bad media."

A smile tilted his lips. His ruggedly handsome face looked exceptionally handsome in the moonlight. Refusing to fall for those looks, she stepped away from him and near the curb to raise a hand at the taxi zooming in their direction.

"Let me take you home." His voice was a husky plea.

Cameron inched further away from the curb, further away from him because she wasn't sure she knew why he wanted to take her home. Was it about her safety or something else? Her mind went back to the way he'd looked at her in the elevator. The intensity behind his gaze was oh so suggestive. No, she wasn't letting Jacob Gray take her anywhere.

Cameron pushed her arm out more to make sure to flag the cab. "You've never lived in New York. This is the way we get around." The taxi stopped in front of them.

Jacob peered in at the driver like he was inspecting the man and taking a photograph with his memory. "I'll get you a car service." He opened the rear passenger door for her. "I'll take care of it tomorrow." He took her hand, helped her inside and positioned the tote bag on the floor's hump. Then he removed his wallet and a bill, knocked on the glass partition between her and the driver and stuck the money in the payment slot. "Text me when you get home, will you?"

"I'll be okay. You forget, I've been in this city for over three years."

"I know, but we'll have to beef up your security especially with this date campaign."

She had misunderstood again. Just like she'd done about the rent. Gray was running a business. Of course her security should be his concern.

He moved the tail of her coat into the cab and tucked it under her thigh so it wouldn't fall free again. Their eyes locked. Cameron had to fight to keep her thigh from trembling. They both felt it, the heat from that connection. She didn't know what it was about Gray and night air. He always seemed to take her breath away when the sun went down and the stars came out.

*The night sky sparkled with what looked like a million stars. Cameron couldn't believe her eyes. A table set with candles, silver and lace in the middle of the forest. They'd already had an amazing dinner and ridden in a horse drawn carriage to get here and now this. "You did all this. How? When did you have –?"*

*Gray cut off her words by pressing his lips to hers. She raised her arms to wrap around his neck and leaned into his firm chest.*

*He broke the kiss, then took her hand and led her to the table. A waiter raised the silver dome. There were three different slices of cake alongside each one was a Tiffany blue ring box.*

*"Let's see if I got it right," he said. "I know your favorite cake or at least I should right? The ring of your dreams should be next to the cake you'll choose."*

*"What if it's not? What if it's next to my second choice?"*

*"Then I'm not ready to be your husband. I'm not ready to make you happy."*

*Cameron took a seat. She stared at the cake slices and the boxes. She wanted him so badly, she didn't care which ring he put on her finger tonight. He was going to ask her to marry him. That's all that mattered. That was all she'd wanted.*

*She reached for the carrot cake in the center and pulled it in front of her. Gray smiled and reached for the box. He got down on one knee and opened the lid. "Cameron Scott would you please do me the honor of making me the happiest man on the planet by agreeing to spend the rest of your life as my wife?"*

*He opened the lid. An impressive princess cut diamond sparkled in the moonlight. Her favorite cake. Her favorite cut of diamond. And now the only man she was sure to ever want in her life was going to be hers. A tear cascaded down her cheek. She nodded, for she couldn't speak. Gray took the ring from the box and slid it on her finger. She leaned closer to him and kissed his lips. "I love you," she whispered.*

*"I love you."*

*She sat back and stared at her ring. Gray rose from the ground and took the other chair and reached for the chocolate cake.*

*"You know I love chocolate and cheesecake too. What if I'd chosen one of them?"*

*Gray's face took on a serious expression. He shook his head.*

*"We wouldn't be engaged, because the other boxes are empty."*

"Your stop."

Cameron opened her eyes to the driver's voice and found herself in front of her building. "That was fast."

"No traffic tonight. Just us and the stars," he replied.

She reached for her wallet. Then remembered Gray had already paid him, so she pushed open the door and stepped out. Cameron entered her apartment. Tossed her things on the sofa and went into the sunroom that she she'd converted to a library. She went for the bookend that held up the Bible and a multitude of other religious devotionals she'd collected over the years and pulled it from the shelf. She twisted the head of the puppy shaped bookend off and removed the blue Tiffany box. She then slid the balcony door open and stepped outside. Cameron looked up at the sky. The stars were like tiny diamonds taking turns glittering as if they were beckoning her to choose them, as if they were slices of cake that offered a promise.

Cameron pushed back the lid to the box and removed the small piece of paper that was folded inside. She had three weeks before the pawn shop she'd taken it to would take possession.

She looked up at the moon and said, "I should let it go." She waited for a response from the moon, the stars, her conscience, God. She heard nothing. "I should have let it go a long time ago." This time she knew she hadn't been talking to anyone or anything but herself.

She folded the paper and returned it to the box. Gray's ring. Gray's promise. Everything she'd ever wanted and hoped for had been destroyed in one night and if her memory served her right on that night there hadn't been a single star in the sky.

# Chapter 13

The campaign to win a date with Cameron Scott was a huge success. Cameron did a round of appearances on most of the early morning and late night talk shows, *Ellen, The View, The Tonight Show* and not a day went by that she wasn't on a radio program. Mary made a decision halfway through the campaign to cap the ticket sales and to her utter surprise they had sold more than forty thousand dollars worth. The final event was a black tie party held at the studio that included the staff from the show, a few big donors, the media and representatives from the Ethan Wright Foundation.

Nearly all the proceeds for the fundraiser were going directly to the charity, so the final presentation of the check was a big deal, but more importantly, the drawing for the date with Cameron was all the chatter on social media.

Cameron slid on her dress for the evening. It was a gift from designer, Herve Leger, a cherry red, tailored dress, with a plunging bustline and asymmetrical seams that fashionably reminded Cameron of bandages. It clung to her figure like Herve had planned to mummify her in it. Her Jimmy Choo Mime pumps in mirrored gold leather complemented the dress. No matter the color or occasion a good pair of metallic shoes always did the trick. She completed her look with beautiful jewelry from Gucci.

"How you maintain that body on the food you eat I'll never know." Stacy commented while zipping Cameron's dress up.

Cameron stepped closer to the mirror and inspected

herself. "It's good genes. All the Scott women have them. You should have seen my grandmother before her stroke. She could have held her own with me any day."

Stacy shook her head and looked up and down at her own pencil like, lacking curves figure and said, "That's a crime."

Cameron shrugged. "A nice body can be a blessing and a curse." She stepped back and patted her hair. "Do you like my makeup?"

Stacy nodded. "You look fab as always."

"My hair?"

Stacy raised an eyebrow. "Double fab."

Cameron sighed. "I think I'm just nervous. I'm afraid some crazy man has won a date with me."

Stacy laughed out loud. "Girl, you are ever the glass half empty chick. I'm going to need you to believe some hot celebrity won. You know a few ballers purchased tickets."

"Yeah, Common tweeted he purchased a bunch of tickets," Gia, her makeup artist interjected.

Cameron turned up her nose. "Common, I mean he's fine and all but he's a little long in the tooth to be trying to date me isn't he?"

"Long in the tooth. Girl, you are still so country. He's only what, like fifteen years older than you? Maybe sixteen or seventeen."

"Old enough to be my daddy."

"He's fine and rich, so he's never too old. But you don't need his money. You have young, fine and rich right here in the building."

Cameron's eyes cut to Gia who wasn't paying attention to them. She shushed Stacy. She didn't want everyone knowing about her and Gray.

"Fine, rich and your age-ish," Stacy teased. "Anyway, if it don't work out with old Lonnie Jr. you can pass him to me and I'll get real common with him."

Cameron laughed. "You know you're crazy don't you?"

"I know I'm trying to get somebody rich and handsome to date me."

There was a knock at the door. Then it opened. A woman from Mary's team stepped in and said, "We're ready for you. I have instructions to take you out the back so you can get in the limo and come around front."

*Smoke and mirrors*, Cameron thought. She picked up her evening bag and shawl and followed the woman out of the room.

Lights from cameras flashed as the media rushed the rope to get a shot of Cameron when she stepped out of the limo. She stopped and posed. Hands on hips, chest out, chin up and right leg extended the way she had been taught to do by her publicity coach back during her days on *Saved Man*. She smiled and walked the red carpet like the pro she was and entered the building. Gray was waiting for her just inside the door.

"I see you're already ready for your date." He offered her his arm and escorted her into the room adding, "You look amazing. I'm starting to think I was crazy to let Mary talk me into this."

Cameron had been smiling for the cameras, but now she was also smiling to herself. "The wardrobe people are good at their jobs."

"You give them too much credit. I think you'd look great in a paper bag."

Cameron spotted Winnie Walker. The woman was

charging toward her. "Then you should save some money and test that theory one day," Cameron said. She gave Gray a playful wink, released his arm and moved to meet Winnie halfway.

"Cameron Scott. You look fantastic." They air kissed and Winnie pulled back. "Are you ready to meet Mr. Wonderful?"

Cameron pursed her lips. "I'm ready for this contest to be over. I sure hope I don't end up with a troll."

Winnie waved a hand. 'Diva, you have to be positive. I have a feeling about this. I think you are going to have a date with your Mister Right."

Cameron waved over Winnie's shoulders at a group of magazine journalists she recognized. "I hope so."

"You're a Christian, girl. You need to have more faith," Winnie whispered. "I sure hope that dreamboat you were just walking in with has a few tickets in the bowl. Who was that?"

Cameron cleared her throat. "That's the Managing Producer for the show. Jacob Gray."

Winnie gave Jacob a thorough once over from the back. "He's fine. Is he married?"

"I'll let you interview him and find out," Cameron replied, pulling Winnie's arm and hoping to dump her on Gray.

"Wait," Winnie said. "Let's take a selfie. I need to tweet that I'm at your event."

They posed for a few pictures. Cameron interrupted Jacob's chat with Phyllis, introduced them both to Winnie and disappeared into the throng of people in the room.

After an hour of appetizers and virgin cocktails or mocktails as the TCT people called them and impromptu photo sessions and micro-interviews with the media, Mary took the stage to begin the short program. She had remarks, Winnie had remarks and Ethan Wright and a few of his board members thanked TCT for their generous donation. Then it was the moment she'd been dreading, the actual drawing. A large glass bowl was in front of the room with thousands of white slips of paper. She was called to the podium where she made a few funny remarks about how hard it is to find a good man. Air filled the bowl and the mixing of the tickets began as the contents swirled around. Cameron fought to keep a smile on her face, but in truth she found this entire contest to be embarrassing. Last year she was on *Saved Man* competing with other women for a man and now she was being raffled off to a man. This being in front of the camera stuff was getting old. She was going to have to rebrand herself or she'd always be the single gal on the show trying to get a man.

The bowl stopped and one of the kids Ethan invited stuck his hand in the bowl and pulled out a winning name.

Cameron couldn't help it. She closed her eyes tight for a moment and prayed it was someone sane and good-looking. She opened them and noticed Timothy Thompson was laughing. "Well, I'll be doggone. I knew all those tickets he was buying were going to pay off. Cameron has won a date with Jacob Gray."

Her mouth dropped open and then she quickly closed it before every photographer in the room got a shot of her tonsils. Rapid heartbeats coincided with perspiration that broke out all over her body. *Gray.* No way!

Jacob walked to the front of the room and stood next to Cameron while the photographers took pictures. He took the microphone and made some speech about never expecting to win, but wanting to give to his best friend's charity. Cameron tried to still her racing heart and her racing thoughts about having to fulfill this obligation, but she couldn't. Gray was still talking and before he handed the microphone to her, he said, "I feel like the luckiest man in the world." A muscle leaped in his jaw. The look in his eyes said he meant every word and that scared her.

Winnie slid next to her and whispered, "Well, it looks like Jesus done showed up and showed out. That's what I call a date for Cameron Scott."

# Chapter 14

Cameron had a vice grip on her dinner bag, but it was no match for the pinched look on her face. Her chest was heaving up and down like a bull that had seen red. She was way past angry. She was mad.

"The good news is you're not having dinner with a psycho."

"I know you rigged this somehow," she hissed through clenched teeth.

Jacob laughed and angled his thumb toward his chest. "Me? Are you accusing me of cheating?"

"You're darn right I am."

He laughed again. "Why would you think I wouldn't win?"

"Fate isn't that cruel," she said taking a sip of her drink. "What are the odds?"

He shrugged. "They're pretty good if you pad the bowl. I purchased a lot of tickets. More than I care to ever let anyone know."

Her eyebrows furrowed disbelievingly. "But there was Marcus Westbrook and a bunch of other athletes who came in at five thousand a pop."

Jacob nodded. "Sorry to disappoint you but I wasn't having you spend the evening with Marcus or any other athlete."

"I'm not disappointed. I'm just saying."

Jacob shrugged. "I know those guys so I called them and asked if I could take their names out of the running."

"What?"

"They were just looking for a tax write off. They weren't really trying to holler."

Cameron cocked her head.

"It was just me and the commoners and I dominated that bowl."

"You seem really pleased with yourself, but you know you're a scam artist. Those other men never stood a chance."

He cast her a sideways glance and said, "You call it scam. I call it strategy. I just played the odds."

She smirked. "Be creative and call it what you like."

"I'll also call it an answered prayer, especially since you won't go out with me any other way."

Cameron avoided his eyes. "This one date is not going to change my mind about that."

"We'll see," he said.

"You should move on, Gray. We've had our time."

"What are you talking about? We're too young to propose we've had our time at anything."

The look she gave him was infinitely remorseful. "We're divorced and if that isn't a sign that a relationship has run its course I don't know what is."

Jacob cleared his throat. "Yeah, you know about that divorce." He hesitated for a moment and decided to man up and get it out. "I didn't file the papers."

Cameron's shock was all over her face; her body language was rife with it and although most people were clearing out, he immediately regretted telling her in this public place. "What did you say?"

He hesitated again, allowing his eyes to sweep the room to make sure all the reporters were gone. "I said, I never filed the papers."

"But I signed them. We signed them."

"Sticking signed papers in a desk at home doesn't a divorce make."

She shook her head. "Are you kidding?"

"I am not."

He wondered if that was surprise or real anger he saw in her eyes when she asked, "How could you do that? I thought I was divorced from you. I was engaged to Rick."

"And aren't you glad you didn't make a bigamist out of yourself?"

"Gray!"

He took the cockiness out of his tone. "Look, I'm sorry. I couldn't do it. I put them away and decided to wait and see what happened and I was right. Look what happened. You broke up."

Cameron crossed her arms over her chest and shook her head.

"So," he said, "how about next Friday night?"

"Don't be smug. I swear you can't do anything without being manipulative."

"Cameron…"

"No. You promised to love and honor me. You promised to take care of me five years ago and now you come back like your leaving was nothing."

He couldn't believe she had the nerve to say that. "You do a really good job of playing the victim you know that.

You act like I did you wrong or something. I'd think you'd appreciate the fact that I still wanted you to be my wife."

"I'm not interested in being your wife. In fact, after this stunt, I never want to see you again." She stomped off in the direction of the elevator and pushed the button. He followed and slid into the car with her. "Leave me alone." Her tone pleaded. He noted her eyes were wet.

"I can't leave you alone and you don't have the option of not seeing me again. I'm your boss."

Cameron whipped around. "I don't have to do this. You don't have me trapped. This contract was issued to me under false pretenses."

The elevator pinged and the doors opened, but neither of them moved.

"So, what? You're going to quit?" He hadn't meant his tone to be teasing, but it was and it wasn't lost on her. She shot daggers at him with her eyes before stepping out of the elevator. "Cameron, come on. Let's be mature about this. If you quit how are you going to take care of yourself?"

A hallow of dim light illuminated the hall. Jacob followed her to the area where the offices were housed and then into her dressing room.

It was he who was pleading now. "Talk to me."

When she looked at him her eyes were still wet. "I can find another job. I'd rather dance on a pole than work with you."

"And validate what I said about you five years ago."

Cameron flinched. Neither of them said a word for a moment. Even more than he was regretting telling her they were still married, Jacob was definitely wishing he could take those words back.

"You're the devil, Jacob Gray. You and your entire

family." She turned her back to him and began to gather her things. She moved quickly, but he could tell by the way her hand was trembling that she was furious.

He grabbed her arm, turned her toward him. "I'm sorry. I shouldn't have said that."

"Please leave me alone." Cameron snatched her arm out of his grasp.

"Cam, I'm sorry. Calm down. If I had thought having dinner with me would cause all this, I wouldn't have done it. But I mean, its Ethan's charity. I have to give to somebody. I just thought I could…" he paused. "Do you really hate me this much?"

Cameron shook her head. "I don't hate you. I just don't believe in second chances."

Jacob studied her. He could see she meant what she said and it surprised him. "Isn't the doctrine of second chances the core of your faith, our faith?"

Sadness filled her eyes. "I don't know how to answer that, but a second chance with you and I would never work."

"You really believe that. I can't understand why."

"It doesn't matter if you believe it or understand. If I'm going to do a good job on the show I need you to promise me you'll keep our relationship strictly professional."

Jacob nodded. "I can do that. Right after the date and right after…"

Cameron's eyes questioned him.

He took a step closer. "Right after this." He dipped his head. Just when he was about to capture her mouth, Jacob heard someone clear their throat behind him. They both turned to find Mary standing in the doorway.

"I started my career as a reporter with Gossip Magazine," she began. "I hated working for that rag… all the snooping and digging up dirt. It paid well, but it wasn't for me. However, there was one thing I learned from the job that I've never forgotten and that's how to read people at a party and know when it's time to eavesdrop on a juicy conversation."

Mary stepped further into the room and leaned against the makeup table. "You two made my antennae go up and I couldn't get them to go down." She paused before asking, "Did I hear what you said correctly? You two are actually married?"

Cameron shook her head. "It's news to me, Mary. I had no idea."

"I think I picked that up." She crossed her arms in front of her chest. "Jacob, what kind of real drama do we have going on here?"

Feeling like a teenager caught making out, he took a few steps away from Cameron. "We were married five years ago and we've been separated about that long."

Although she'd obviously learned this when she'd been standing outside the door, Mary still looked shocked. "Why don't I know that? Why is it a secret?"

Jacob wrinkled his brow. He didn't have an answer to that so he didn't answer. Cameron was mute as well.

Mary however, had plenty to say. "You need to understand my issue here. We just ran this fundraiser and you conveniently won a date with your own wife. We could have people say it's rigged. They could want their money back."

"But I purchased a ridiculous amount of tickets."

"I would have hired an accounting firm if I knew." Mary crossed her hands over her chest and shook her head like the number of tickets he'd purchased didn't matter. "I can't work without information. In my business, I've got to know what I'm dealing with."

Cameron finally spoke. "Do you think it'll be a problem?"

Mary twisted her lips the way she always did when she was thinking hard. "I don't know. But it's possible someone who knows you were married could come forward and say so."

"What do we do?" Cameron asked. "How can *Jacob* fix this?"

Mary was thoughtful for a long moment and then said, "We leak it. We get in front of it and spin it ourselves."

Cameron shook her head. "He's my boss."

"We'll say you were trying to protect your privacy. No one will care that he's your boss. This business is full of nepotism."

Cameron rolled her eyes at him.

"The show is *Second Chances*," Mary said. "Jacob wants a second chance. My gut says run with it, but this is a hard one. I have to figure out how to make it work." She stood and walked to door. "I'm rarely surprised, but you two…" She finished her statement by wagging her finger. "I'll see you in the morning." And then she was gone.

Cameron let out a long breath before speaking. "I won't quit the show and I obviously have to do the date, but I have one request."

Jacob asked, "What's that?"

"File those divorce papers." She attempted to walk past him, but he grabbed her arm. She stopped, looked in his eyes and her mouth parted like she was going to say something, but then closed as if she changed her mind.

"I'm sorry I didn't tell you earlier." He let her arm go. "Let me take you home."

She looked at him strangely for a moment and then shook her head. "My friend is here."

"We need to talk."

"Gray," Cameron yelled his name. "Please stop."

"I can't," he replied. Had he just begged? He swallowed his shame and took a few steps back. Where was his pride?

Neither of them spoke, nor did they meet each other's eyes. He broke the silence by clearing his throat. "Friday night. You may as well get it over with."

She raised her eyes to his now. He forced a smile. Something like panic flashed in her eyes. She was afraid of him. His gut told him it was a good fear, fear of being alone with him. All this protest was protection mode.

"I've got to go." The words came out just above a whisper. Then she said goodnight and walked out of the room.

He took a seat and sat there a long time, hoping and praying that after next Friday she would never leave him again.

# Chapter 15

"There's no other way to do this."

Cameron felt like she'd been zapped with a taser. "Are you telling me you want me to pretend that Jacob and I are back together? That I've given him a second chance?"

"I'm not one to ask someone to lie, but this is a media nightmare waiting to happen. The truth is going to come out. We have to spin it our way or the media will slaughter you. The show will be ruined. We won't recover."

Cameron dropped her head in her hands. This was a disaster. "What were the other scenarios?"

"To leak that you were married and let you respond you didn't know you weren't divorced. But it won't work."

"I'm not sure I see how this is much different."

"In this picture, we have a happy ending. We don't have you going off and filing divorce papers without giving your husband a second chance. You're a Christian. That's what we do right?" Mary paused a beat and continued, "In my scenario, we tell the truth. You were out of work. Jacob came back to the United States like a knight on a horse and saved his estranged wife from eviction and ruin. He wins the date and you go off and have an amazing time. You summarily grant him his second chance. We even announce how much money he spent winning the date. It's romantic. Women will love it. People will be drawn to it. We all love the rich, handsome prince that comes in and saves the girl."

The story sounded good in theory, but Cameron wasn't

sure how well it would actually go over. She was sick of being in the media. Housely, rumors of losing her job on *Heart*, which were true, but still rumors and the eviction. She hated this and she said so. "I don't like it. I'm not sure I can do it."

"Cameron, you put on a show for a living."

"But this is Jacob, Mary. He's my…we have history."

Mary's tone carried an empathetic lilt. "Of course you do, but right now we're trying to take care of the present and the future, so I need you to rise above the past."

Cameron sighed. Mary made sense, but she still had to pull it off. "How long would we have to pretend we're a couple?"

"Not long at all. We'll release the story and then you have the big date. We'd need you to be seen in public a few times before the Hunter Perry episode airs and both of you would have to commit to not dating other people through the summer. You don't have to be dating each other, but no one else either."

"Won't people want to know if we're together?"

"You pull the privacy thing. Questions about your relationship are off the table, because you're working on it, etc., etc. You're entitled to do that."

Cameron was thoughtful. She wasn't convinced this would work and she said so. "Are you sure we can't just hope for the best?"

"I'm afraid not. I've dealt with this a hundred times. It's always a mistake to hope for the best. As it is, we may have to give some of the donation money back. But at least we can make the news story about a second chance. I'm confident it will help the show. Your audience, which is largely made up of Christian viewers, will forgive it."

"Have you talked to Jacob?"

There was a knock. "That's him now." Mary stood and pulled the door open. Jacob walked in. He looked tired and annoyed. Cameron had heard through the grapevine that he'd gotten an earful from the Thompson execs about not fully disclosing the details of their relationship. He greeted her. Then he took a chair.

Cameron felt bad for him. She knew Jacob had a good heart. He never did anything with the intention of doing harm, but still she didn't respond. She wasn't feeling it.

"That's not very good practice for being my wife." Jacob's tone was sarcastic and gruff.

She shrugged. "It's practice for an unhappy wife."

"We're not going for the unhappy look." He frowned and leaned forward in his seat.

The two of them faced off in a short-lived battle of wills. Jacob conceded first. "I'm sorry. I really am, just do what you do and this will work out."

New annoyance flitted through her. "Do what I do? What do you mean by that?"

"Pretend and be charming," he said firmly.

Cameron rolled her neck. She was ten seconds from letting him know what she thought of him, but Mary interjected. "Is this about the current situation or something else?"

Neither answered. Jacob's eyes softened. "This is me taking my frustration out on the one person who doesn't deserve it."

Cameron let her eyes slide in his direction.

"Look, it's not a big deal in terms of your personal life. It's not like you're seeing anyone, right?"

He asked the question casually, but it was the fear in his eyes that told her how much the answer actually meant. "That's none of your business."

"Technically, it is my business. And legally…"

"Legally, so I'm legally still your wife and that makes it your business?"

"You have a morality clause in your contract. Being married and still looking is grounds for termination. Thompson will enforce it. They just informed me of that."

Cameron sighed again. Why was she fighting with him? She wasn't dating anybody. And she had to remember why she was here in the first place. She needed a job. The entire situation was becoming exponentially more difficult to tolerate, but it was going to secure her and her family's future. "I apologize. You are paying me well, so you're right. I'm a happy wife. Just let me know what I need to do and I'll do it."

Jacob raised an eyebrow. "You didn't answer the dating anyone question."

She smirked. "No. I haven't had a date since Housely."

"And there wasn't much dating before him," Mary threw in. "Just escorts to events, right?"

Cameron nodded and realized how embarrassing that was.

"Great. You come across as a good girl and that's what we need." Mary smiled. "You're a trooper. I knew you would be." She stood. "I'll have someone from my team get with you later to coach you. You're going on Jimmy Kimmel tonight and I can't think of a better time to announce it."

Cameron groaned. "Tonight? I haven't even had time to process all of this."

"The sooner you make the announcement, the better,"

Jacob stated. "Kimmel is a good guy. He'll handle it well."

Cameron guffawed. "That's easy for you to say. You won't be on live television making the announcement."

Mary threw up her hands. "Separate corners folks, please." She looked at her wristwatch. "I've got to run. Let's meet for dinner. I'll coach you though the Kimmel stuff myself."

Cameron agreed and Mary made her exit.

A beat of silence and then Jacob said, "I wish I could take your place tonight, babe. Please believe me when I tell you I really am sorry. I tried to talk Mary out of this approach, but she reminded me that even though we eloped and didn't really tell a lot of people, that folks in the county clerk's office and people at the hotel and apartment complex we lived in…those are our viewers. They add up."

She nodded. "It's not a problem. Like you said, I'm good at pretending right?" She stood. "I'm going for a walk. I need some air."

"May I join you? It could be a good photo op."

"I need to think. I'd prefer to do that alone." She reached for the door and stopped. Without turning to face him she said, "Gray, I understand what I have to do. We'll walk tomorrow, okay. Just let me have today. I need to get my head together."

Jacob nodded and Cameron left the room.

***

Meetings with Mary and her team had become as frequent as showers and so had the constant attention of the paparazzi.

"I know the last couple of days have been rough," Mary began, "But any publicity can work for you, even what we perceive as bad publicity." She looked at Cameron and then continued. "The show has gained thirty thousand likes on Facebook this week and we have another twelve thousand people following us on Twitter. That's a lot of growth. Your stats are up as well, Cameron."

Cameron rolled her eyes. She was trying to be courageous about all this, but the negative social media comments and emails were nasty. They were outnumbered ten to one by positive feedback, however the negative always stood out more. People accused her of misrepresenting herself. Rick Housely made it worse by releasing a statement claiming her secret marriage was the reason they'd broken up. She roared inwardly. She could have choked him for adding to the chatter. He was forever the opportunist.

She was becoming messy, one scandal after another. Cameron seemed to be attracting drama and that wasn't who she was or what she wanted for her life.

"We've contracted with a brand management company," Jacob said interrupting her thoughts.

She raised her head and then raised an eyebrow at him.

"They'll work on helping you establish a brand."

"I thought I had one," she said.

"Not really," Mary interjected. "You had the start of one, the makings of something, but not really anything solid. This company will fix that. You'll work with them next week a bit, but the bulk of the work will happen during the filming break, before you make all the media rounds."

"Before the season begins," Jacob added.

Cameron nodded. Her eyes filled with tears. She'd just read a really nasty tweet that called her a slut for going on *Saved Man* when she was still married.

She'd made the announcement on Kimmel as planned, placing more of the responsibility on Jacob for her not knowing she wasn't divorced. Mary's team figured he could take the hit, but it didn't matter. Jacob was behind the scenes. Nobody cared about him and too many people decided that if Cameron didn't have copies of the final divorce decree she never should have been on *Saved Man* hunting for a new husband.

Of course there was public sympathy for the other side. Lots of people came out and shared their own stories about not having known they weren't divorced. One woman even spoke of winning the lottery and having to share it with an abusive ex-husband she thought she was divorced from. Cameron appreciated those stories. Still, the negative energy was strong and as much as she tried to keep it from getting her down, she knew she had no one to blame for this mess but herself. She hadn't made sure that she and Jacob were actually through. She hadn't made sure for the same reasons he said he hadn't filed the papers. She couldn't. And the impact of that realization bothered her. She cast a glance in his direction. Why couldn't she?

Mary peered over her eyeglasses. "You should let Stacy manage your social media for awhile, or I can get someone in my office to take care of it."

"Stacy is handling it." Cameron raised a finger and wiped a traitorous tear that had fallen. "I keep punishing myself by looking. Don't worry. I'm fine. I'm just tired."

Mary swiped a few pages on her iPad. "I have some more good news. It's been three days and not a single soul has asked for their money back from the drawing."

"People love what Ethan Wright is doing. I'm sure it was more about the charity than it was about me anyway."

"Thankfully, it appears that way. The good news is the more days that pass since the story was released the less likely they'll be any financial fall out."

Cameron and Jacob nodded.

Mary stood. "I have some more work to do and you both have a big night tonight. You need to get some rest and be prepared to deal with the paparazzi. The city crawls with them on Friday nights."

Mary left the conference room. The two of them sat in silence for a long time.

"Cameron, I'm sorry," Jacob said. "I really made a mess of this."

She shook her head. "So you've said every day this week. I said I'm fine."

"You're crying and that's breaking my heart."

"Well un-break it," she snapped. She took the temper out of her voice. "I've been through much worse. Crying is the way I release stress."

He steepled his finger beneath his chin, "I would never intentionally hurt you or your reputation. You know that right?"

She knew that. God, she knew all too well. "I think it would have been a little better this week if Rick hadn't made that statement."

"Can I ask you a question?"

She sighed and waited for it.

"Why did you go on *Saved Man*?"

A sound of dismay escaped her lips. That came out the blue. "What do you mean? It was a job."

"But when you auditioned for the show you were married."

"You sound like the folks who are tweeting about me."

"I'm not judging you. I'm asking."

She shrugged. "It was a paycheck, Gray. I never expected to get that far. I didn't expect to win."

"So you weren't looking for a man?"

"I was trying to pay my bills." She picked up her bottled water and took a sip. "I'm always trying to pay my bills."

He nodded like that answer pleased him. "You accepted his ring."

"That was for show. For the show."

"You're sure he never cared about you?"

"Did you see today's Daily News? Does it look like he ever cared about me?"

"I guess I find it hard to believe that any man could get that close to you and not feel something."

Their eyes connected for a moment. Cameron saw the heartfelt meaning in his words. She shrugged. "Maybe a straight man would."

Gray dropped his hands. His chin nearly hit the table. "Huh?"

"Yeah," she replied. "Possibly bisexual, but he definitely likes men. I'm sure of that."

He was stone cold shocked. "Wow!" He laughed and Cameron couldn't help it, she laughed a little too.

"Housely is a joke. I just wish I hadn't been his punchline."

Gray tapped a pointed index finger on the table. "Maybe you should out him. After the lies he told this week, he deserves it."

Cameron had considered fighting back, but she figured it would only make things worse. She didn't repay evil for evil. "Not my style," she offered with a smile. "But I know things that Housely does not want the rest of the world to know."

Gray's voice teased her. "She's not crying anymore."

Cameron blushed. It felt good to laugh, even if it was only a chuckle.

"I could tell you some stories about my adventures overseas that would have you in stitches."

Her lips crooked into a half smile. "Then I guess that will give us something to talk about while we're pretending for the next month or so." An easiness that made her uneasy settled into the room. They spent more than a few seconds looking into each other's eyes. Cameron broke the stare by standing. "I have a couple of radio interviews that start soon."

He nodded and gathered his things. "Six-thirty sharp okay? The beginning of the evening is time sensitive."

"I'm sure it is, because you never change."

"I hope that's not a bad thing."

She decided to leave him in suspense on that and walked out of the room.

\*\*\*

The rest of the day sped by in a blur and before Cameron realized it she was looking at six-fifteen on the clock.

"You look fantastic!" Stacy reached for the bottle of perfume and released a spray at her back.

Cameron turned and gave her the evil eye. "I already did that."

Stacy put the bottle down. "Not enough. I can barely tell you put it on."

"Forget the perfume." Cameron turned to face the full-length mirror. "He'll be here in a few minutes. Are you sure this dress is okay?"

"Girl, what? If he wasn't already in love with you he would be before dinner was over."

Cameron turned her head and gave Stacy another flash of evil. "I told you. I'm just trying to get this over with. I'm not interested in Gray being in love with me."

Stacy smirked. "Too late for that. He's already all in."

Cameron stepped back from the mirror and pulled at the spandex laced fabric that was glued to her size six hips. "This is too sexy," she said walking to her closet. "I'm going to wear the white and black."

Stacy leapt in front of her. "I forbid you to wear that church mother dress on a date. Where did it come from anyway?"

"It's a dress I actually do wear to church and there's nothing wrong with it."

"Everything is wrong with it. The only man's attention you'd get in that dress was one who'd been in prison for the last ten years. You will wear what you have on. Remember, this isn't just about you and Jacob. This is about the show. Paparazzi will be taking pictures. You have to look snatched."

Cameron closed her closet door and fell back against it. "You're right."

"I know. Now let's pick a sexier shoe and a sexier pair of earrings and get you down to the car before Mr. Perfect gets bored waiting."

"Gray is not perfect."

"Well, technically none of us are perfect, but he's close."

"A man that left me is close? You may need some higher standards."

"Let's be real. Being pregnant by somebody else does fall in the realm of being a leaveable offense." Cameron opened her mouth to speak and Stacy cut her off. "I know the story, but I'm saying, Jacob doesn't and I'm not sure that's all his fault. If you opened yourself up to loving him again, you two could work it out."

Cameron sighed. "I think you forget about my daughter. She complicates this and that's never going to change."

"It might not be so complicated if you told him the entire story."

Cameron waved her off. "Please don't annoy me before he gets here." She walked to her jewelry vanity and sifted through her collection."

Stacy joined her and said, "No ma'am. Go into your safe and get those earrings Housely gave you."

Cameron rolled her eyes, "Girl, I sold those to make a car note."

"That sure was a lucky pawn shop. They've got all the good Cameron Scott jewelry."

"It was easier to part with it than you think."

"Well, I can think of one piece that you seemed to have a hard time letting go."

Cameron knew she was talking about her wedding rings. She hated when Stacy was right. It wasn't that she wore them, but at one time they'd meant the world to her. She also knew Gray paid a fortune for them. It seemed criminal to let them go for so little.

Stacy cleared her throat. "Are you planning to get them back now that you're working?"

Cameron ignored that question. "I have an idea. How about you do some assisting and wade through this and help me choose."

"You don't have to get all snitty with me. I was just asking. You know I have savings. You could get your rings back and pay me back when you can."

"I appreciate your offer, but I'm sure those rings will make some other bride very happy. I am getting a long overdue divorce as soon as Mary tells me it's okay."

Stacy groaned and mumbled words of disagreement as she picked through the jewelry. Cameron selected a pair of metal spiked stilettos and tousled her hair some more. She had just put the earrings in that Stacy selected when the doorbell rang.

"I told him to text me when he arrived."

Stacy crossed her arms over her chest. "Apparently, Mr. Imperfect at least has perfect manners."

Cameron smirked. "How did he get past the doorman?"

Stacy's eyes widened. "I might have left his name at the door."

Cameron shook her head. "You'll be here when I get home?"

"Of course. Leigh's man is back."

"Am I good?" She ran her hands down her side.

"Fabulous." After a moment of misty eyed staring, Stacy pulled Cameron into a hug. "I know he hurt you. You hurt each other, but please just…try to have a good time tonight. Just a good time. You really deserve that."

Cameron closed her eyes tight and fought the sudden

desire to wish for a good time to come true. *This is business*, she told herself. She stepped out of Stacy's embrace and granted her a conciliatory smile. "I'll try."

"No talking about work, or checking Twitter and no fighting about the past."

"Okay. I've got it."

Undeterred by Cameron's tone, Stacy continued. "Try to be with the man you dated in college. Before you got married and things went horribly, disgustingly, disastrously wrong. I mean wrong on steroids."

Cameron raised a hand to stop her. "I get the point. I'll really try to at least have fun." She turned and left the bedroom. Stacy followed, but went into the kitchen where she wouldn't be seen from the foyer.

Cameron pulled the door open and fought to close her mouth. Her fingers froze on the door knob. Her eyes swept Jacob's body from head to toe and then back up to his face. Gray was dressed in a black, three piece suit. It was a slim cut that fit close against his well shaped body. The cream dress shirt and caramel paisley silk tie made his hazel eyes appear ethereal and sunkissed. Her breath caught. He looked amazing. He smelled like trouble. Cameron was sure to melt under the potency of his sexy cologne.

He seemed to be mesmerized by her as well. His eyes swept her body from head to toe several times. Neither said a word for nearly thirty seconds. Jacob cleared his throat and raised the bouquet of flowers he held. "I know roses are nearly a cliché, but I also hope they're still your favorite."

Excitement danced in her belly as she took the flowers. "Thank you. They are still my favorite." She raised them to her nose sniffing the fragrant petals. "I'll put these in water." She rushed from the door and entered the kitchen.

Stacy gawked and then took the flowers from her hand.

"Nice. He didn't pick these up off the street."

Cameron reached into the pantry and removed a crystal vase. "Put them in water, please."

"I'm going take pictures and put them on your Instagram."

"Whatever, I won't know until I get home because I won't be what?"

"Checking your phone and acting distracted," Stacy replied.

Cameron left the kitchen, picked up her clutch from the hall table and returned to the foyer where she'd left Gray. "I'm sorry. I didn't really invite you in, did I?"

"I do need a minute," he said pulling his hand from behind his back. A black bag dangled from the tips of his fingers. He offered the bag to her. "I think this will go with your dress."

Cameron swallowed hard. *Flowers and a gift*, she thought. He was trying hard. He was winning.

He pushed the door closed. "Did you get the flowers in water? That was really quick."

"Stacy is here. She'll take care of that for me."

Stacy peeked around the corner and waved. "Hello, Mr. Gray."

Gray stepped toward her and extended his hand for a shake. "I've seen you on the set, but we haven't been formally introduced. Nice to meet you, Stacy. Please call me Jacob."

Stacy blushed like she was meeting Omari Hardwick instead of her boss and then pulled herself together and said, "I'll go see about those flowers."

They entered the dining room. Cameron opened the

bag and pulled out the heavy box. She opened the metal clasp that secured it. Inside was a diamond necklace and matching earrings. She was speechless, but she did utter his name. "Gray."

"In the spirit of coming clean, I have to tell you this came out of my publicity budget. I'm not in the position to spend this kind of money on jewelry right now, so you actually have Mary to thank for approving my request." He paused. "But, I did pick it out. If the thought counts for anything, I spent hours looking at pieces."

Cameron hadn't stopped staring at the beautiful necklace. He couldn't have made a better choice. He'd always known what she wanted. All these years and he still did. She smiled, turned her back to him and lifted the hair off her neck. "Would you put it on for me?"

Gray closed the space between them. She could feel the heat from his body and the warmth of his breath on the back of her neck as he removed the necklace she was wearing and replaced it with the one he'd picked out.

He put his hands on her bare shoulders and teased her collar bone with his index fingers. Simultaneously, their eyes followed the path to their reflection in the mirror on the wall across from them. He whispered, "It's perfect."

Mesmerized by it's beauty, Cameron raised a hand to finger it. She agreed.

A light flashed to their left. "I'm sorry, but this seriously needs to go on Instagram," Stacy exclaimed.

Jacob laughed and let go of Cameron's shoulders. She removed her earrings and replaced them with the ones that matched the necklace.

"Another shot?" Stacy asked. They posed for a few more pictures. "Cameron has strict orders to have fun tonight."

Jacob turned. His eyes did a naughty sweep of her body. "I think I'm up to the job."

Cameron cleared her throat. "Now I know we need to go."

"Yes, we do," Jacob replied. He extended his elbow.

Cameron looked into his eyes and hesitated for a moment. Then she slid her arm through his and they exited the apartment.

# Chapter 16

*There was hope,* Jacob thought as he observed the look on Cameron's face. She hadn't stopped touching the necklace. He hadn't seen that look of surprise since the night he proposed to her. She was also shocked when they arrived at the airport. He was glad he hadn't tried to go the safe route. Using the Thompson Jet was exclusive, intimate and luxuriously impressive.

"Where are we going?" she asked.

He grinned. "You know me. It's a surprise."

Cameron eyed him suspiciously. "I assumed we were staying in the city."

"You also know me better than to make assumptions."

"How far are we traveling?"

Jacob laughed at her persistence. "Not far, but don't worry. I've got everything covered."

"You don't know what I'm worried about."

"The weather, your shoes, any number of things that you women like to know before you get on a plane, but I've taken care of it." He stood and walked to a small closet behind them and removed a long garment bag and handed it to her.

She laid the bag across the table in front of them and stood to pull the zipper. The first item out of the bag was a full length faux fur coat.

"I know you posed for PETA, so real fur is out, but

this is on Oprah's list of her favorite things."

Cameron frowned. "We're going some place cold?"

"Some place a little colder than the city." Jacob sat down, but this time he claimed the chair next to the one she'd vacated instead of across from her.

She raised an eyebrow, removed the coat completely from the bag and examined it. Once again, her eyebrow went up when she spotted the name of the designer in the label. "This is nice. Really nice."

"Consider it a party favor."

"I've already got the jewelry."

"The jewelry is my way of saying I'm sorry for all the aggravation."

She moaned, pulled the coat off the hanger and slid it over her body. "It's a perfect fit."

"Of course it is. You're the exact same size you were when I met you."

Cameron took off the coat. Jacob let his eyes linger over her body for a moment. He'd lied a bit. She'd gained a couple of pounds, but every single one of them had landed in the right place, especially the ones on her behind. He turned his eyes from her before he got caught staring.

She reached inside the bag and removed a pair of sneakers. She chuckled. "Really, Gray, am I going running?"

He shrugged. "You never know."

She reached in and pulled out a pair of ballet flats. This time she cocked her head.

"You're a woman. You need choices." He smiled and reached for the glass of wine he'd poured himself.

Cameron put both pair of shoes down on the table and reached back in again. This time she pulled out a small case.

She unzipped it and removed some toiletries and a tightly folded nightgown and then she looked down and gasped at what he assumed were underwear.

"Don't worry. My assistant picked that stuff out. I have no idea what color those drawers are."

She smirked. "I am not staying out all night with you."

"Just in case something happened and we had to get a later flight in the morning. I wanted you to be prepared."

She reached into the bag again. She didn't remove them, but he knew she was looking at a pair of a jeans and a sweater, because that's what he'd requested.

With the exception of the coat, she put the items back in the bag. "So where's your emergency gear?"

Jacob nodded in the direction of the closet. He noticed she looked less than pleased. He took her hand and pulled her down onto her seat. "Cam, I'm not trying to disrespect you. I was just hoping we could spend the night and at least do a tour before we head back. You'll understand why when we arrive."

She relaxed a little but removed her hand from his. "Is there a reason you're sitting so close?" she asked giving him a peripheral eye roll. "There are plenty of other seats on this plane including the one you *were* sitting in."

"What's the matter? Do I make you nervous?" He leaned closer.

This time she faced him and gave him a strong look. "Don't flatter yourself. I just like my personal space."

He stood. "I promised you I'd be on my best behavior." He walked to the bar and picked up the wine bottle he'd opened. "You seem a little tense. Are you sure I can't interest you in a glass of wine?"

She shook her head, turned to face the window and

simply said, "I don't drink."

"Too bad. I thought it might take the edge off."

She turned back to look at him. "Don't tell me you're nervous."

"Never that. It was your nerves I was concerned about."

Cameron closed her eyes. "As long as you don't get a buzz and forget this is business."

"You promised to have fun."

"I'll be cool if you'll be cool, but remember this…I don't do remixes. This is work fun. This is about the show."

The overhead speaker came on and the captain announced that it was time to fasten their seat belts for their approach to Niagara Falls airport.

# Chapter 17

"I don't do remixes," Cameron repeated the words in her head as the limousine pulled onto the most beautiful property she'd ever seen in her life. She read the name: The Excelsior Fallsview Resort. "I don't do remixes," she whispered under her breath.

"What was that?" Jacob asked.

"I said I've never seen the falls."

"Neither have I," he said, softly. "Remember, we said we'd go on our first anniversary?"

She did remember. How could she forget? All of her plans and dreams dissipated when he disappeared. Her entire world imploded.

The limo stopped in the enclave of the hotel. The driver opened the door for them and gathered their bags.

A white-gloved gentleman dressed in a black suit met them at the hotel entrance. "Mr. Gray, welcome to the Excelsior Resort. Madame Scott-Gray. My name is Samuel and I am your concierge. Please let me escort you to your suites."

Gray took her hand. Cameron frowned a bit. *Scott-Gray*, she thought. He'd taken some liberties with her name, just like he was doing with her hand, but she didn't fight her first thought which was to pull away.

The hotel was elegant. She'd stayed in some swanky places since having a bit of television fame, but she'd not stayed anywhere near this classically posh in her entire life.

"I trust you had a good flight," Samuel stated.

"We did," Jacob replied. He and the man made small talk about the amenities available at the hotel and the various places he and Cameron should visit before they left the area. The way he was going on, one would have thought she and Gray were staying for a week.

The elevator ride was long. When it finally stopped, they stepped out onto the thirty-third floor. Cameron counted and noted there were only six doors on the floor.

"The View Suites as you requested, Sir." Samuel opened the door and Cameron's mouth fell open. The open floor plan gave them a panoramic view of the falls from the door. It literally took her breath away. She stepped into the room with Gray close behind. This time it was she that took his hand as she pulled him to the floor-to-ceiling windows. The falls were illuminated in colors: pink, yellow and turquoise. Fireworks exploded over the water in a festive pattern that charged the atmosphere, even in the room.

"Incredible," she whispered gleefully. She looked up at Jacob and smiled.

"Sir, Madame," Samuel said from behind and they turned. He offered them both champagne glasses.

Cameron thanked him, but didn't accept. She returned her attention to the falls, because she wanted the drink. Badly. She'd wanted the one Jacob offered her on the plane. Being alone with Gray was not going to be easy.

Gray put his arm around her shoulder and she noted his other hand was empty. He wasn't drinking either. She appreciated that.

"Let me give you a tour and then I'll be out of your way," Samuel stated. "You've already seen the view." He extended his arm to the right. This is the View Room. It has an outdoor balcony with a fireplace. The windows open so you can hear the water if you like. You'll dine there, so I'll allow you to explore that during dinner." He walked a few feet to the right. They followed him to a suite of rooms. One included a small library with various books by bestselling authors and a picture book collection of the falls. They entered an entertainment room, which included a massive television and theater seats that looked so comfortable Cameron was sure they'd rise to meet her body.

They exited the media room and walked back past the great room. Samuel showed them the kitchen and then moved on to the bedroom suite.

"I'll allow you to tour the bedroom on your own." Samuel backed out of the room and closed the double doors behind him.

Cameron thought she'd never seen such a magnificently furnished suite. The room itself was cream. The California King Platform bed was the centerpiece. It sat on a walkup platform that was trimmed in various shades of gold, shimmering tans and taupes. But what really made the room special was the eclectic selection of Native American paintings and accent pieces.

The over-sized bathroom extended into the main bedroom with a glass enclosed Roman tub that was set against the windows so it had a clear view of the falls. Like the great room, the view of the falls was spectacular.

Jacob cleared his throat. Through her peripheral vision, Cameron could see him stick his hands in his pants pocket. He rocked back on his heels. "Looks like a honeymoon suite."

Cameron agreed but didn't say so.

"Remember that suite we had for our honeymoon. It was a roach motel compared to this."

"It was perfect," she said. Cameron quickly regretted

how easily that slid off her tongue.

Jacob smiled appreciatively. "At the time, I thought it was the best room in the entire world especially since it had that whirlpool tub." He chuckled at the memory. "But I guess it was the company and the occasion."

Cameron continued to be mute. She bristled a bit when she thought about how they'd made love in every corner of that room and multiple times in the whirlpool tub. They'd barely come out for food.

Samuel was waiting for them when they stepped out of the room. He handed a set of keys to Cameron. "This is your room, Madame. Sir, you are just through here, he said opening the door to a connecting suite.

"I'm sure it's fine," Jacob said pocketing the keys Samuel handed him. "But I'll let you know if I need anything."

A bellhop entered the room with their bags. Then he and Samuel left them alone.

Cameron put a hand on her hip. "Connecting suites?"

"It's all they had," he replied. "It was short notice. I just won last week."

"Uh, huh." She grunted, dropped her evening bag in a chair and walked out to the View Room, which was bathed in flickering candlelight and warmed with a roaring wood burning fire.

Jacob removed her coat and let his hands linger on her shoulders for a moment. He whispered close to her ear. "I know the past six months have been difficult for you, so I want you to relax and enjoy this trip."

Cameron turned her face away from him, but he took a finger and pulled her chin back toward him. "You can have anything you want, Cam. Just tell me what you need and I'll make sure it's provided."

*Anything she wanted*, she thought. He meant it. She could see it in his eyes. He'd do anything for her. She thought about the implications of that. Thought about how in the past few months there had been times when she'd gone to bed hungry because she'd had her fill of peanut butter and ramen noodles, the only food she could afford. Now here was Gray, wanting what he'd always wanted for her…the best that life had to offer. She tried hard not to let "the best" of this world be a high priority item for her, but it was nice to have a man that wanted her to have it. It was nice to have someone else looking out for her. It was nice not to be the one who shouldered all the responsibility, all the time.

Choked up with emotion, Cameron swallowed. An "Okay" escaped her lips. It was the only word she could manage to get out. He was standing so close and the view of the falls from the balcony was so beautiful and romantic that she had to admit, the only thing she wanted right at that moment was to thank him in a way that meant something. That's what she told herself, but maybe she wasn't being honest. Maybe she just wanted a kiss. Her mouth parted. Her eyes landed on his lips and then went back up to his eyes. Cameron could tell he knew. Yes, he knew and like always, Jacob Gray didn't hesitate to give her what she wanted.

# Chapter 18

The kiss was long and passionate and intense. When it was broken by both of them Jacob moaned, "God, Cam, I've missed you so much." He pulled her into his arms and let his hands drop to her lower back. Her body melted into his. Jacob wasn't sure if he was going to be able to keep his promise that he would be a complete gentleman tonight to her or to himself. He lowered his lips to her ear, then her neck and whispered it again, "I've missed you, baby."

Cameron stepped out of his embrace. Then moved a few more steps away so she wasn't standing so close to him. "We've been in here less than five minutes and you're already getting out of line."

"It was just a kiss."

That wasn't just a kiss. Was he on crack? That had been an explosion. She raised her hands to touch her slightly swollen lips. She'd gotten what she wanted and now she couldn't handle it.

"I won't do it again," he said. "Not unless you ask me to, but I'll say this, that was worth putting up with your wrath for the past month."

She didn't respond.

"Did I tell you how incredible you look in that dress?"

She lowered her eyes. Wringing her hands she said, "You're teasing me."

"I'm being honest."

"You're making this hard."

"It didn't seem like it was so hard a minute ago."

"Okay, I kissed you, but that's it. We can pretend for the cameras, but you know we can't actually date."

She'd flipped the switch on him again. He had no idea how she managed to do that so seamlessly. He grunted. "We don't have to date. We're married."

Cameron pitched an eyebrow. "Married? There is absolutely nothing God ordained about a couple who hasn't even talked to each other in five years."

"Are you sure?" he asked. "Are you sure that this entire reconnection wasn't ordained by God?"

Cameron hugged her elbows. Jacob could tell she was about to get really defensive. "No, it was orchestrated by you. I thought we were divorced. I had moved on."

He refused to let her off the hook. "You say that, but I don't know. No papers, sweetheart. You never checked for papers."

"Papers or not, I'm not going to pretend I have an interest in being your wife, because I don't. I don't even know you anymore and I can tell you for sure that you never knew me, so please let's go eat and try to keep this where it's supposed to be."

"Where is it supposed to be when two people love each other?"

"You're assuming." Cameron laughed bitterly. "That's so like you."

"Are you saying you don't feel anything for me?"

"I'm saying I don't want to have this conversation. I don't want to fight with you."

"I'm not trying to fight, Cam. I'm trying to handle the

119

way I feel about you in a mature manner."

"What, by controlling me? You offer me a job you know I can't not take and then you buy up all the tickets to a contest to force me to go on a date with you. You've manipulated and controlled me ever since you came back into my life."

"Wow!" Jacob snatched his head back. "Manipulative and controlling. Here I thought I was being assertive."

"Aggressive is more like it. There's a difference."

"I don't get points for at least being creative?"

Cameron deadpanned him.

"On the matter of that job offer, I'd think that wouldn't be a strike against a brother. It cost me a fortune, nearly my entire fortune to fund this show."

"I didn't ask you to do that."

"You didn't have to."

She expelled a sharp breath. "Let's be honest. Was the show about me or about you?"

"It was about us."

"That was a big gamble to take with your future on a whore you couldn't trust the first time!" She yelled. Those words sucked the fight right out of him.

Jacob whistled. "Okay, so are you finished now? You cut me appropriately with my own nasty words, said in anger might I add about a situation that warranted it. Now can we do what we agreed we would do for tonight...leave our past trespasses in the past?"

Cameron shook her head furiously.

Jacob threw up his hands and pulled a chair out for her. She looked at it like it was cursed or something and said, "I need to use the restroom." She disappeared through the door and down the hall.

Jacob waited nearly twenty minutes for her to return. During that time dinner was delivered and set up. Cameron reentered the room. Her swollen eyes told the story her body language was trying to hide, she'd been crying.

He stood. "I'm sorry."

"I need to tell you something," she said. "I need to tell you who Charity's father is.

He groaned inwardly so hard that she probably felt the tremor. "Before I eat?"

"You need to know."

He sat back down and took her hand. "I want us to just start from now. From today."

She snatched her hand back from his. "Do you realize I have a daughter? Like the fact that she's not here doesn't mean she doesn't exist. The fact that she's not in New York City, doesn't make her any less real."

"Not knowing who her father is has nothing to do with me acknowledging her." He swallowed before speaking. "In fact, I'd like to meet her. That's why I asked you about her before."

She denied his truth. "No, you don't."

"You think I'd hold something against an innocent child?"

"You did when I was pregnant."

"I left you to be with your new man."

"Sure you did. That's why you paid the rent for a year, so some other man could live off your money?"

"I paid the rent because it was cheaper to write the check than have the discussion about whether or not you needed it. I wrote the check to clear my conscious so I could do what I did which was disappear and bleed in private."

Cameron raised her hands to cover her ears. Jacob reached for both her hands and pulled them way from her ears. "I wrote the check because I don't abandon my responsibilities."

She grunted.

"What was that for? I don't abandon my responsibilities, unlike this guy did. Where is he now? Was he worth it? Has he ever done one single thing for you or your daughter?"

She shook her head. "No, he hasn't. But he's dead, so you know he can't really pay any child support."

"Dead." Jacob paused a beat then said. "I'm sorry for your daughter."

"Don't be," Cameron said, standing. "He was an S.O.B. and most of the time when I think about him I hope he's in hell."

Jacob's annoyance dissipated a bit. "You don't mean that."

Cameron's eyes filled with tears. "Yes, I do."

"Well, let's talk then. Go ahead and tell me what you wanted to say."

She cut him with her smile. "So now it's okay for me to tell you what I wanted to say, because it's convenient for you to learn it. You don't feel threatened any more. No worries about the whore lying back down with him."

He popped out of his chair. "Stop saying that."

"Whore, whore, whore!" Rage filled her. "That's what I'll always be to you, so I'm not going to play this dating game."

Jacob groaned and threw his hands up in surrender.

"You can enjoy the dinner and the view from your own room. Let me know when you're ready to take the flight back to the city."

She went to her bedroom and slammed the door.

# Chapter 19

Cameron kicked off her shoes, plopped down on the bed and cried for nearly thirty minutes. Then she did what she always did when she felt alone. She tried to pray. But prayer wasn't helping her tonight. She didn't really want to hear from God. She just wanted to dump her issues. God's plan included love, forgiveness and a spirit of self-control. Cameron was full of hate, unforgiving and steaming mad. She wasn't even sure why. She called Stacy.

"It's a disaster."

"What happened?"

"I'm in a room. We're in a hotel in Niagara Falls. We had a horrible fight." Cameron's shoulders shook. She started sobbing again. "I can't be with him, Stacy. I just want to go to work and earn my check and not deal with this."

"Okay, I get it. I just…" Stacy paused. "Cameron, I can't help thinking that some of your issue with Jacob isn't about him."

Her voice hitched on a sob. "What do you mean?"

"Honey, you were raped. You never really had much counseling because you quit going. Don't you think it's possible that you're going through what other victims of rape go through?"

Cameron was silent. The word rape caused such a pain in her heart she wished someone would take her out of her misery.

"Rape victims sometimes blame themselves and they

feel unworthy of love. I can't help but think that some of the reason you haven't told Jacob is because you're afraid. You're afraid that he'll hurt you worse than you're already hurt by rejecting you because of the rape or he'll blame you or some other crazy thing men sometimes do."

Cameron shook her head. This emotional rollercoaster ride he had her on was unnerving her. It was making her crazy. She wanted a drink.

"Cameron," Stacy called. "Do you hear me? Is any of what I'm saying making sense?"

"I don't know. I…I'm just tired. I've been trying so hard. I used to try to date, but I just couldn't…"

"Honey, I'm your best friend. I've been watching you avoid this pain for years. Please get some help."

"He'll think it was my fault."

"Why do you believe that?"

"Because I know he will."

"I think he'll believe you."

*Nobody is going to believe you,* the voice in her head said.

She closed her eyes and squeezed tight.

Her mother's voice, *What did you do?*

His voice, *Look, I got carried away. You're not hurt. He doesn't even have to know.*

Her mother's voice, *I told you to not go gettin' involved with those rich people. They're different. You know how they treat women like us.*

Cameron put her hands over her ears and tried to drown out the sound of the voices. She needed a drink.

Jacob's voice, *I can't believe I married a whore.*

She heard a knock at the bedroom door. She cringed.

She wasn't ready to deal with him. Hadn't she banished him to his own suite?

"I'll call you back, Stace." She ended the call, crawled off the bed and pulled the door open. A woman was standing there. She entered the room and rolled a dining cart in. "My name is Sonia. I'm from concierge services. Mr. Gray asked me to bring dinner."

Cameron nodded. Sonia rolled the tray into the room. She began to arrange the food on a table. "No, please. It's fine. I can serve myself."

Sonia nodded. "Is there anything else I can do for you, Mrs. Gray?"

*Mrs. Gray.* No one had called her that in years. She wasn't Mrs. Gray. They had split up before she even officially changed her name on her driver's license. She looked around at the room and thought about Gray dining alone after all the trouble he'd gone through to bring her here, but she couldn't be with him. She couldn't try again like he wanted to. She felt a familiar pain in the pit of her belly and then she heard the voices again. *Whore. Nobody will believe you. What did you do?*

She squeezed her eyes shut. She knew how to drown out the voices.

"Are you okay? Can I get you something? Perhaps, Mr. Gray?"

"Yes, you can get me something. I'd like…" she paused for a long time. Painfully considering the impact of the words she was about to say. "I want a glass of wine."

The maid smiled like she was glad she could do something for her. Cameron caught a glimpse of herself in the mirror on the wall. Her mascara was running. She looked a mess. *Do you think he'll take your word over mine?*

"What kind of wine would you like?"

"Anything, white or blush, please. I prefer something sweet."

*Women like us.*

"Yes, ma'am." She went to the door and pulled it open.

"Wait, I'm sorry. I don't remember your name."

"Sonia, Mrs. Gray."

*Mrs. Gray. Whore.*

"Sonia, bring the bottle, okay."

Sonia nodded and walked out the door.

Cameron stepped back and let her body fall on the bed. "Just bring the entire bottle."

# Chapter 20

Jacob fell back on the bed and pushed the button on the remote. He'd spent a fortune for this evening, fifteen thousand for the charity and ten thousand for the flight, limo and hotel and all he'd done was make Cameron angrier than she'd ever been. He could have done that for free, right at the office.

He flipped the channels a few times, looking for something interesting to watch. If he had any pride he'd have gotten their things and her and flown back to New York City tonight, but he had no pride. He was a hopeful fool. He was holding out hope that she'd wake in the morning and miraculously decide she wanted to be with him.

He chuckled. "Fat chance of that happening." But then he remembered 'With faith all things are possible.' He also remembered his name. He was Jacob and Jacob would wrestle all night with an angel until he got what he needed. He wasn't giving up on himself. He wasn't giving up on his wife.

But even as he declared he'd fight, he realized his mistake. It was the same one he made years ago. He hadn't allowed her to talk. He hadn't let her tell him about the other guy. It infuriated him that she wanted to. Didn't she know the thought of another man making love to her the way he'd made love to her made him absolutely insane? Why didn't women understand how deep that cut a man?

He flipped the channel again and couldn't believe what he was seeing, a rerun of *Saved Man*. It was the episode when that punk, Rick Housely, presented Cameron with the final flower and the ring. He couldn't bear to watch Housely touch her. Gay or not, the guy couldn't keep his hands off of her throughout the entire season. It was the most painful television Jacob had ever watched in his entire life, but he didn't miss a moment of it. He couldn't tear his eyes away from her face, her lips, her eyes. Even if all those parts of her belonged to another man.

Housely started his speech about how much he loved her. As sick as it made him, he always watched it with the same interest, the look on Cameron's face. For a woman who had beat fifteen other women out of one of America's most eligible bachelors, she didn't look that happy. He could see it in her eyes. She didn't love him. He could see that now. It was all for show just like she'd said. That made him happy, but the joy only lasted a few moments, because he realized her not loving Housely did nothing to further his own cause. She didn't love him either. She'd made that painfully clear hours ago when she slammed that bedroom door and didn't come back out of the room.

Jacob turned the television off. He looked at the wall clock. It was close to eleven p.m. He and Cameron were supposed to have had dinner and now be walking arm and arm through the tourist district. He groaned. He blew it and as assertive as he thought he was or aggressive as she perceived him to be, Jacob knew when he was beaten. There was no way he was going to fix this mess tonight. He stood, changed out of his clothes and stepped into the shower.

***

Jacob thought he was dreaming, because every night when he went to sleep he dreamed he was making love to Cameron, but this feeling on his chest and his thigh was not a dream, these hands were real. So were her voice and the wisp of breath against his ear.

"Wake up, Gray."

His eyes popped open. In the dim moonlight bouncing off the falls outside his window, he could see her face hovering above his. Her voice was breathy when she spoke. "I want you to make love to me."

His mind struggled to register her words. Just hours ago she'd been angry enough to push him off the balcony and now she was in his bed asking for sex.

Cameron blinked, but other than that she remained perfectly still. Her ebony eyes shimmered in the darkness. She tilted her head and smiled sexily. It was then that he realized, she meant what she said. Blood started rushing to every extremity in his body. "Cam, what are you talking about?"

Straddling his body, she answered him without words. Naked as the day she was born, she leaned down and pressed her lips against his. That's when he tasted it. That's when he smelled it. Alcohol. He took her by the waist, careful not to touch any other part of her naked form, lifted her off of his lap and sat up. "You've been drinking, baby. I thought you didn't drink."

Cameron took a finger and swiped it across his lips. "You think too much. I did not come in here for your brains." She straddled him again and began kissing his face and neck and bare chest.

Jacob groaned and fought to keep his body from responding. "Baby, look, I know you think you want this, but I'm not going to be able to do this while you're drunk," he said moving his head back and forth to avoid the heat of her lips on his.

She lowered her hand and touched him between his legs. "You're wrong. I can tell you, you are up to the task."

She giggled mischievously.

He closed his eyes and moved her body off his again and stood. He did a half turn so he wasn't looking directly at her. All that chestnut brown flesh was so tempting. She was right about his body's response. It was taking every ounce of strength and self-control that he had to not give her what she was begging for, what he was begging for.

"What's wrong?" she asked standing up on the bed. She placed her hands on her hips and danced around. "You don't like what you see?"

"You need to put some clothes on. Where's the nightgown thing I got for you?"

"It's in my room. I don't want to put on clothes. I want you to make love to me the way you used to when I was your wife for real. Remember that, Gray? I can still do that little trick you taught me."

Jacob forced temper into his voice. "Cam, stop playing. I'm going to get you a robe. Don't move because you could fall off the bed and hurt yourself."

He rushed into the bathroom and grabbed one of the guest robes off the hook behind the door. When he returned, Cameron was sitting on the bed Indian style with her face buried in her hands. He took the robe and wrapped it around the back of her. He pulled her hands from her face and took one of her arms and pushed it into the robe. Then he pushed the other into the other sleeve.

Jacob realized he was perspiring like he'd worked all day in the hot sun. He wiped his forehead and whispered, "Thank God."

Cameron was curiously quiet. He turned his head, finally able to really look at her now that her body was covered.

"Why don't you want me, Gray?" Her words came out

slurred, but even with that she sounded like a little girl who was hurting.

He shook his head. "I do want you. I want you more than I want anything in this world, but I can't have you like this. You've been drinking."

"Not that much."

"I think you've had quite a bit."

She got quiet again, and then said. "I should go back to my room."

He took her hand. "Please don't. Stay here with me. No talking. No fighting. Just us lying together. Can we do that?"

Cameron nodded. She slid back on the bed. "I can't sleep in this hot robe."

He popped up off the bed. "I'll go get the gown. I'll be right back."

She nodded and he left the room. Afraid this moment with her would disappear if she sobered up completely, he practically ran through her suite. When he reached her room, he found the bag and pulled out the nightgown. He left the room, but not before noting the two empty wine bottles on the table. She had really put it away. No wonder she was acting so wild.

He went back to the room. When he entered she stood, "Thank goodness, I'm boiling." She opened the robe and let it hit the floor.

"Oh God, Cam," he said turning his head. He stepped sideways until he felt her take the gown from his hand. Jacob kept his back turned until she told him she was done. Then she slid back on the bed. "Can I have some water?" she asked.

He went to bar and poured her a glass. "You sure you don't want coffee?"

She smiled and accepted the glass from his hand. "No, I'll need that in the morning."

She took a few sips, placed the glass on the nightstand and pushed her body down under the duvet. Jacob went around to the other side of the bed and climbed in with her.

He was nervous. He hadn't been this nervous in a long time. He was close to her for the first time in years and as much as he appreciated the fact that they were going to be intimate without being intimate, he knew this was going to be the hardest night of his life. He opened his arms and Cameron spooned in against him. He moaned inwardly and wrapped his arms around her.

She twisted her head sideways in his direction and asked, "You sure you don't want to take me up on my offer? A drunk whore is just as good as a sober one." She pulled away from him a bit, closed her eyes and it seemed she instantly fell asleep.

*Whore*, he thought. Was that what was between them? Was the fact that he called her that horrible name going to keep them apart forever? Why couldn't she get over that? He was here trying to get over the fact that she'd slept with another man. Why couldn't she forgive him? He didn't understand.

He lay there for an hour or so, staring at her. He thought about all the women he'd been with since they'd separated. None of them made him feel the way he felt when he was with Cam. No one had even gotten close to holding his attention for more than a few weeks.

*I want her back*, he thought and the decision was made. No more let's try again. Let's see if we can work it out. He was playing for keeps. He felt the Holy Spirit stir and the words; *with faith all things are possible* ministered to his soul. Jacob knew all things were possible, because not more than an hour ago he was lying here alone and now he was holding her like they'd never spent five years apart. God was working it out for him. His job was to not mess it up.

He pulled Cameron closer and started to pray. He asked God to show him how to take the power away from all the angry words they'd said to each other. He asked God to open his heart and help him to hear her the next time she wanted to tell him something about the past. He asked God to help him accept her daughter and he asked God to help him not be prideful, because even though she hurt him horribly, he still loved her and he needed to forgive her completely so they could begin anew. He prayed what felt like fifty prayers, quoted every scripture he knew as he held his wife and just when he was about to fall asleep, Cameron turned her body toward him, opened her eyes and whispered the words, "I still love you, Gray." His heart started pounding in his chest. She closed her eyes and fell back asleep just as quickly as she'd awoken, but no one could tell him that in that moment when she uttered those words, that she was not sober.

# Chapter 21

Cameron woke in Jacob's arms, spooned against his body, smelling his scent and feeling his bare chest against her back. The other thing she felt was the crud in her mouth. Last night's wine was like sludge. It was a taste she hadn't had in three years, but it was familiar. She'd been drinking and now she was in Jacob Gray's bed.

She moved a little. Jacob moaned. Then he did her the hugest of favors and rolled away from her onto his back. She lifted the comforter and took a peek at him underneath. She sighed with relief to find he was wearing pajama bottoms and that only the top half of him was nude. She glanced at his chest for a moment and realized she'd forgotten how nicely made he was. Well, she hadn't forgotten. She just hadn't let herself think about it. He had the Greek letter for his fraternity branded on his chest. The image looked larger now, but she noticed it was because his chest seemed broader. Gray was working out and he'd filled out more over the five years since she'd seen him.

Cameron sat there watching his chest rise and fall and thought she could watch him breathe for hours. *What kind of sick realization was that?* She asked herself, but she couldn't tear her eyes away. Her bladder, no doubt full of wine helped her to realize she had to move. She carefully inched away from him, slid her body off the mattress, and took quiet steps to the restroom.

She relieved herself for what seemed like an hour then used the courtesy dental supplies on the counter. After which, she spent a ridiculous amount of time staring at the falls and trying to remember how she'd ended up in Gray's bed. Cameron heard a light tap on the door, reached for the robe on the hook and slid it on before telling him to come in.

Jacob entered the room. He was holding a coffee mug in his hand, which he offered to her. "You've been in here a long time. You're not sick are you?"

She raised the mug to her lips and blew on the hot liquid. "I was looking at the view."

"You had a lot to drink last night. Two bottles of wine."

Cameron shrugged. "Now you see why I don't drink." The image of her mangled car and the upside down car seat on the highway came to her memory. "I haven't had a drink in three years. I won't have another. I realize last night was a mistake."

Jacob nodded. "The drinking brought you to me, so I'm not sure I agree."

Cameron took a long sip from the mug. Her stomach cramped and she put it down on the counter.

He took her hand. "You must be hungry. Let's get dressed and go have some breakfast."

She looked down at their hands. Her first instinct was to remove hers from his. He must have sensed it because he locked his fingers a little tighter and gave her a tug that pulled her from the bathroom.

Thirty minutes later, Cameron joined him at one of the hotel restaurants. Minutes after she sat, breakfast was delivered.

"I ordered," he said. "I hope you don't mind."

The waiter put down all her favorite breakfast foods and served tea, her breakfast beverage of choice. She took a sip, looked at the spread and said, "You remembered."

Jacob picked up a carafe and poured a glass of orange juice. "I remember everything about you." His eyes bore into hers for a moment and her stomach tumbled. "I'll say the blessing so we can eat."

Cameron was surprised by the spiritual changes she'd seen in him over the past few weeks. He opened their meetings with prayer, always said grace and prone to an occasional foul word in the past, he had completely cleaned up his language. He attended church on all the big holidays and a few more times a year because she expected it of him, but he was not religious or spiritual. He certainly didn't pray.

"You seem changed spiritually," she said.

"I got saved a few years ago."

"Tell me what happened. How did you cross over?"

"I was in Africa with Ethan. I met him when I worked on a documentary with CNN. I was really drawn to this guy who had so much light in his spirit. I was kind of in a dark place. I'd lost my mom and my brother. Grief had me twisted. My mother had been sick, but Justin's death was a shock."

Cameron's gut clenched. She tried to speak, to offer condolences but words didn't come out. Gray didn't notice her current state of muteness, so he continued. "I'd been doing a lot of risky things; racing cars and jumping out of airplanes, filming in some pretty remote and dangerous parts of Africa. I don't know, I guess I really didn't want to live much, but Ethan did. He introduced me to Jesus in a way that took the focus off of me and what I needed. His focus was on ministry and service. He was so blessed. I had to learn more."

Cameron's heart stopped at the thought of Gray risking his life, but she made herself smile. "Ethan sounds like a good friend to have. I'm happy for you, Gray. I mean, Jacob."

"I like it when you call me Gray."

"I know, but I'm just trying to…"

"Keep things professional? You woke up in my bed, in my arms this morning. You're still my wife, Cam. And right now, that means something to me. So we're way beyond being professional."

A pretty blonde passed their table so closely that her leg brushed their tablecloth. She apologized and gave Jacob a flirtatious wink. He nodded but quickly returned his attention to Cameron. Images of him and other women flashed through her mind and her brow tightened. "You've been running around with women for years. I've seen some of the pictures, so, when did me being your wife begin to mean something to you?"

"When I realized none of those women would ever fully satisfy me because they weren't you."

Her stomach tumbled again. She dropped her eyes to her plate, cut her pancakes and put the first mound in her mouth and chewed before saying, "Speaking of waking up in your bed. How did that happen?"

"I didn't lock the door between our rooms so I guess you wandered in. I was sleeping, no doubt dreaming about you and suddenly you were there."

"I climbed in your bed."

"Yeah, pretty much. Not before stripping naked though."

Cameron felt her cheeks burn. "I did not."

"Oh yeah, you was sporting what your Mama and a good trainer gave you. And by the way, you've done an amazing job of holding on to that banging body of yours."

She continued her protest. "I was not naked."

"If you say so."

She was mortified. Alcohol. That's why she stopped drinking. Too many crazy things happened after she got intoxicated.

"I've always believed the saying, 'a drunk man tells no tales.' You got drunk and sought me out. That speaks volumes, girl. That let me know what's really in your head. You're fighting me consciously, but subconsciously you want the same thing I want."

She pursed her lips and rolled her neck sistah style. "Maybe it was my libido. I mean, you are fine. That hasn't changed."

He chuckled lightly. "Maybe, but my gut tells me it was more. I'm not going to push it though."

They ate in silence for a few minutes and then he asked, "The drinking, is it a problem?"

She shook her head. "It used to be, but it hasn't been for a very long time. Years. I won't let what happened last night happen again."

He nodded. "I understand. I had a few nights where I had more than I should. As long as you know how to put the brakes on…"

"I do," she said. "I definitely won't let the word get out that I'm a drinker. That's the last thing the show needs."

"I'm not asking for the show. I want to make sure you're okay."

Warmth filled her. She smiled and said. "I'm good."

"Great," Gray exclaimed. "Since we're still here I was hoping we could start our date over and take in the tourist sights."

"You went through a lot of trouble. I can't say no." Cameron paused a beat and then said, "I'm sorry I got so upset last night. I'm really sorry I called you controlling."

"You meant it, but it's under the Gray blood."

"The Gray blood."

"Yeah, that's the stuff I've forgiven," he chuckled. "Let's let this date be about today. Pretend I'm some construction worker from Brooklyn who paid fifty bucks for a ticket."

Cameron laughed. "I can't do that."

"Why?" he asked pushing out his chest. "Those construction workers are pretty buff."

"It's not that. I...we have too much history for me to pretend you're someone else, but I can have fun. I can live in the moment with you."

Jacob clapped his hands together loudly. "Now that's what I'm talking about. Commitment. I'm going to hold you to it."

Cameron smiled. "I'll be good. You'll see."

# Chapter 22

And she was good. She was fun. She went to all the tourist spots on his list, which included the wax museum, Adventure Theater, and Old Fort Niagara. They even did a helicopter tour and some outlet shopping since it was obvious they would be spending at least one more night in town. It was during the shopping that Cameron was recognized. She signed a few autographs and took a few pictures. Then they decided their day out in public was over.

They went back to the hotel and rode the elevator to their suites. They went to their respective rooms, showered and changed into the clothing they'd picked up during their shopping. After which, they met in Cameron's living room. She was convinced that Gray would look good wearing anything. He'd slipped into a fitted cranberry sport shirt and some slacks. The color was vibrant against his skin, but still masculine enough to make him look like he'd stepped off the pages of G.Q. magazine. He offered his elbow. Cameron took it.

Her heart was pounding a mile a minute, but she managed to say, "You've been such a gentleman."

"It's the southern boy in me."

They traveled to the roof top restaurant, were greeted and shown to a private dining room.

Cameron was struck by the décor. Vases of purple roses filled the room. Petals were on the floor, the chairs and tables. Candles were lit in nearly every space they could fit and John Legend piped through the speakers. Even the falls had cooperated, because they were illuminated a dark lavender color.

His name was the only word that would come out of her mouth. She closed her eyes to keep the tears at bay. He was doing it again. Doing what he had done the entire time they'd courted years ago. Gray was going the extra mile to make her feel special and it was working. Cameron hadn't felt like this in more than five years. "It's beautiful."

He looked pleased by her response. "I had to compete with those sets on *Saved Man*. I admit Rick's backdrop was always on point."

"Rick had a team of people setting up props for him. Trust me when I tell you he is the least creative man I know." She paused and closed her eyes. She took in the sweet smell of the roses before she opened them again. "Fragrant Plums are my favorite. My grandmother used to grow them."

"And did you think I forgot that?" he asked. He pulled her into his arms and squeezed her tight. "I told you I remember everything."

She released a plume of air and allowed herself to enjoy the moment in his arms. He felt so good. Smelled so good. Made her feel so good. Oh God. She was doing it again. Falling under his spell, the way she had fallen in college. She was such a sucker for romance. It wasn't easy, but she forced herself out of his embrace.

He smiled like he knew the effect he'd had on her. "Let's eat."

They talked about their films and the film business for hours. Gray had the same passion for making great films that he had when he was in grad school and Cameron was in undergrad, but now because he was saved his passion was for making good Christian family films.

"You should acquire some books and have them made into screenplays. Christian novels would adapt well to film."

"Adaptations, I hadn't thought about that really." He paused, seriously considering it. "You might be on to something."

"I am. Trust me. Ready made stories that have already proven to be successful with your target audience."

"You sound like you've given this a lot of thought."

Finished with her meal, Cameron reached for her napkin and wiped the corners of her mouth. "You know it was never my intention to be in front of the camera. That just happened."

Jacob nodded. "I'll have to see if I can help you with that." He raised his glass and took a sip before saying, "I've been talking to the folks at TCT about the movie programming. They know they need to diversify more and the recent success of some holiday films on Centric and TV One has sparked their interest."

"TCT definitely needs to appeal to a younger, female audience. I mean we all like watching preachers and docudramas and stuff, but women want romance. Women want this room. They want this room with a man who loves Jesus, so I'm telling you go for the books."

Gray smiled. "Your passion is contagious. I'll definitely have someone get on the numbers next week and see what that looks like. If it's promising, I can pitch it at the next management meeting."

They talked some more, mostly about his experiences overseas. They had long finished their desert and Gray yawned.

"You're tired," Cameron said.

"A little. I didn't sleep much last night. I had this gorgeous woman hunched up against me and I couldn't make love to her."

This time she wasn't embarrassed, she was grateful. "Thank you for respecting me."

"No, thank you for drinking too much and wandering into my room. You in my arms meant a lot." He face took on a serious expression. "I meant what I've been saying for weeks, about us working it out. I don't want to play games for six months. I love you and that's real."

Her thoughts came to a sudden stop when he said he loved her. She tried to keep the tremble out of her voice when she spoke. "You think we stand a chance? After all this time, with all that's happened?"

"I think today was a good start."

Cameron wasn't so sure. "This place is not our real world. It's bought and paid for and none of the outside pressures of our lives are in it."

"I know that, but what I'm saying is I want to try. One day at a time. One date at a time. Heck, one phone call or text message at a time. That's how people build. That's how they restore trust. One act at a time."

She stood and felt the full gravity of her meal and his words. They were both too heavy for her to digest at that moment. "I'll think about it."

"That's promising." He paused and stood too. "I know we need to talk. I know we might need to get some stuff out in the open. I just didn't want to do it tonight."

"I can't say I blame you. I went a little nuts last night."

"You were honest. Your emotions were raw and that's okay. I want you to be you. I need you to be honest."

He took a few steps toward her, put a finger under her chin and tilted her head up. She dropped her eyes, but couldn't fight his magnetic pull. She slipped under his arms into his embrace. Gray squeezed her tight. Cameron felt the way she always felt, like she had stepped into the arms God had meant for her to lie in for the rest of her life. The thought overwhelmed her and she pulled away.

"What's wrong?" he asked.

Cameron shook her head. She couldn't even describe what she was feeling. "Nothing. I just…one act at time."

A smile tilted his lip. He nodded with understanding.

Desperate to break free of the trance she fell into every time he captured her eyes with his, she pointed to the windows. "Look at those fireworks."

Jacob turned and they both stepped closer. He picked up a remote control the waiter had left with them and pushed the button to open the windows so the sound of the fireworks and the falls could be heard in the room."

"I'm never going to forget this," Cameron whispered.

Jacob put the remote down and took her hand. "I hope not, but give me a chance to impress you for the rest of our lives." He lowered his head. He raised a hand to the front of her neck and used his thumb to massage the base of her throat. Cameron tried to breathe. Following one stuttering exhale, she froze. Waiting for the moment she knew was coming, the moment when Jacob did what he did best.

He lowered his head, tentatively at first like he was testing her to see if she was agreeable. After last night's disaster he was probably pretty unsure. She knew her eyes betrayed her. Her mouth was begging to touch his again. It was like a magnet. She couldn't stop him. She didn't want to.

Their lips met. Cameron turned her body toward him. She let go of her misgivings and melted into him just like she had all those years ago when he'd kissed her for the first time in college. She heard the whistling and then the explosions.

She and Gray broke the kiss just as a huge design illuminated the sky. They watched in silence, but Cameron was barely moved by the display. The fireworks show had nothing on the way the man holding her hand made her feel. She was thrilled and terrified at the same time.

\*\*\*

Cameron sat on her bed listening to music. She thought she was tired when she told Gray she wanted to go to bed. It was nearly midnight after all, but once she changed out of her clothes she felt a surge of new energy. The blinds were up on the window and she watched the falls cascade and crash in a rhythm that only God could have orchestrated. She was trying hard to keep her mind on God, but she was struggling with that. The truth was she wanted a different kind of god. Once again, she wanted a drink. She didn't know how she'd get through the night without one, but she had to do it. Why had she let that demon out of the bottle? She had to be bigger than she'd been last night or her life would start to spiral out of control. Again.

Images of her mangled car came back to her. She was blessed to be alive. Less than sober, she'd crashed head on into another vehicle on I-40. Charity had been in the backseat. The impact of the crash threw the carseat from the vehicle and it landed upside down. Trapped in the car, Cameron had to listen to her baby cry for a full ten minutes before help arrived. The firemen had to cut the car open to get her out. Miraculously, they only had minor cuts and bruises. The driver of the other car had been intoxicated too, but he was good and drunk. Cameron's blood-alcohol test results had been lost, so she wasn't charged with anything other than speeding. But she knew she was partly to blame for the collision. That had been her wake up call.

Her mother had been on her case about the drinking and had even indicated she didn't think Cameron was ready for motherhood. "Maybe you should focus on your career. You should try to see if you can get on a news station in Charlotte."

Cameron's degree from Winston-Salem State University was in mass communications. She'd been making telemarketing calls for the cable company. She decided her mother was right. It was time to stop moping over her failed marriage and do something with her life, especially since Gray had been gone for two years. But Cameron made a decision. She decided Charlotte wasn't where she wanted to be. She was going for the gusto. She was going to New York City.

When she arrived, she found that she was one of possibly a quarter million mass communication grads looking for work, so she tried her hand at acting which seemed to work out better for her even though she wasn't trained. The roles she landed were for extras on soap operas. Then she had several small time commercials. Those jobs and the savings she still had from the money Gray left her were enough to help her make it over the hump until she landed a small continuing role on a soap opera.

She'd gotten lucky, because so many of the actresses she competed with had studied drama professionally. She'd just had one drama class at UNC School of the Arts and she wasn't nuts about acting. Drama sparked her interest in film and that's how she ended up in Gray's film class. He was a grad school teaching assistant, covering their professor for Film 101.

Cameron smiled at the memory. Smiled when she thought about the first time she saw him. He was the most handsome and the most polished young brother she'd ever met. She could tell he was a rich boy. He had money and good looks. All the women wanted him. To her surprise, when he chose, he chose her. Let him tell the story and he'd say he knew she was the woman for him from the first time he laid eyes on her. He proved it. He pursued her. Courted her the old-fashioned way and made her his wife. And now they were here, in adjoining two thousand dollar a night suites, wanting to be together, but sleeping apart. How had the God that made her feel like she was made to rest in his arms for the rest of her life allowed things to come to this?

*You need a drink*, a voice in her head said. She shook off the lie. The last thing she needed was a drink. She was already thinking crazy thoughts. Blaming God for her situation with Gray was so in the loser zone.

She turned over on her stomach and buried her face in the pillow wishing she had a sleeping pill or something to help her relax. Cameron thought about the wine in the refrigerator and the wine and liquor in the bar. It would be so easy to just…but she resolved she would not. "Resist the devil and he will flee from you," she whispered. She'd learned years ago to speak the Word of God to the dark voices. It had worked better for her than any AA meeting she'd ever attended.

She picked up her phone and rooted around for a change in music. Donnie Hathaway's version of *A Song For You* was probably not the right choice, but it touched her soul and made her think of Gray. She let it play twice and then turned off the phone and the lights and pushed her body down under the duvet.

*You need a drink.* The voice in her head was louder.

Cameron closed her eyes tight and spoke The Word aloud again and then said, "I don't need a drink. I want Gray."

Gray made her feel special. But once she told him the truth about Charity's father, he'd never look at her the same again. The truth about Charity's father would break his heart in more ways than one and she'd always be the person responsible for his pain. She was sure of it.

*But I need him*, she thought. I need him to be a husband to me. She'd been lying to herself for years thinking she didn't. If you couldn't be honest in the quiet of the night in your own space with yourself when could you be? It felt so good to wake up with him this morning. She'd missed that feeling over the years. His scent, his warmth, the way their bodies locked together like puzzle pieces. She wanted that one more time. But that wasn't all she wanted. She wanted him to make love to her. She wanted it while she was sober and could remember everything about it.

She pulled the cover back, sat up and stood. Tonight was it. Tonight would be her last chance to be with him that way. Gray wanted her. She knew that wouldn't be true after they talked, but at least she'd have what she needed, a fresh memory of his taste and touch while she was legally and "technically" as he called it his wife.

Cameron stood outside the connecting doors. She knocked once and then opened it. To her surprise, he wasn't in bed. He was sitting in a chair watching television.

"Hey, what's up?" he asked. She took the remote from his hands, pushed the power button to turn the television off and shushed his lingering question with a long passionate kiss. Although he couldn't be accused of making a huge effort, Gray tried to talk some sense into her. "I don't want you to do anything you're going to regret."

"I'm not going to have any regrets."

"I'm not trying to talk you out of this, but I need you to be sure because I can't do another night like last night."

She placed a finger on his lips and said, "Stop talking, Gray." She took his hand. Gray stood and led her to the bed. This time when she asked him to make love to her, she wasn't drunk and he didn't say no.

# Chapter 23

**Could this be love?**

The caption in U.S. Weekly magazine read under the many pictures of Cameron and Jacob that the photographer had shot in Niagara Falls.

"Let's see," Mary said, "We also have **A Second Chance for Cameron Scott**."

**Jacob Gray Wins The Drawing and Wins Back Cameron's Heart, Cameron Scott Reconciles With Estranged Husband**, were some of the others on various news media and blogs.

"This is better than we could have been anticipated," Mary exclaimed. "If I didn't know this was for the show, I'd think someone is thinking about giving her husband a second chance."

"Stop teasing me."

"I'm not teasing. I'm just saying. You folks are looking mighty cozy."

Cameron felt her heart fill up with joy over the memory. "It was a nice weekend."

"Weekend?" Mary's hands went to her hips. "Excuse me."

"We did all the touristy stuff up there, so we stayed over until Sunday morning. In separate rooms of course."

Mary gave her a quick look and smirked. "Yeah, of course. If Jacob Gray was my husband, I'd sleep in a separate bedroom."

"We did have separate rooms," Cameron insisted. Technically, they had.

"Well, even though you had separate rooms it sounds like someone is getting the second chance he wished for."

Cameron felt butterflies fluttering around in her belly. "It was a fantastic date. I've always wanted to go to Niagara Falls. He remembered that. He remembers everything."

"That sounds like true love to me."

Cameron shook her head in an attempt to clear it. "I'd like it if we could get back to work on my schedule."

"If you insist." Mary tapped on her iPad screen. "You know we have next week off. It's Holy Week, so this place is closed."

"Yes, I'm going home. It'll be good to get out of the city," Cameron said, but she was really thinking about how nice it would be to see Charity.

"I didn't know you were leaving town. I have you on the walk-on list for Good Morning New York, but I can move that back."

There was a knock on the door. Mary turned the knob and opened it. She smiled like a high school girl when she saw that it was Jacob. "Cameron and I were just finishing up."

Cameron's eyebrows rose. "No, ma'am, we were not. We just got started," she said pointedly at Mary. Then she turned to Jacob. "What can I do for you, Mr. Gray?"

Mary cleared her throat. "I need to grab a cup of coffee and make a call. I'll be back later." She made a hasty escape.

"Mr. Gray." He frowned. "It's Jacob to everyone in this building and I'm sure I should be on a first name basis with you." He sat on the edge of her desk. "You've been avoiding me all week."

Cameron shrugged. "You're working me like a mule. Have you noticed how much I've been out of the studio filming?"

Jacob's brow knitted. "Are you serious? I've called and texted you every day."

"My schedule has been crazy."

Again he eyed her suspiciously and after a beat said, "I've noticed like this pattern of every third time I text you I get a one word response. Are you counting my texts and responding when you think you have to?"

Cameron stood. Guilty. She was guilty, but she wasn't going to admit it. "Counting texts. You might have too much time on your hands."

Gray let the corner of his mouth go up like he wanted to smile but couldn't manage it. "Did I do something, Cameron?" he asked. The look on his face was sincere, almost fearful.

Her voice became ragged with emotion. "No, Gray. I mean..." She shook her head. She was messing this up horribly for an actor. "Mr..."

"Gray, honey. That's what you call me. That's what you've been calling me since you met me." He took her hand and pulled her body to him. "Why are you running from us? I thought Niagara was special. I thought we connected in a way that would eliminate this weirdness."

"I'm not being weird."

He stared at her for several beats, then put his hand around the front of her neck and used his thumb to move up and down like he was channeling her pulse. "Yes you are. I brought my A game... the planning, the date, and the..."

She raised a hand and put her finger over his lips. "I

know what you did. You don't have to remind me."

He reached for her hand and pressed it into his lips, kissing the fingertips. "I'd like to remind you." His tone was more than a little naughty.

She had been fighting to keep her emotions in check, but he made her blush.

"We've hardly had a conversation since we got off the plane." He pleaded. "I miss you."

Cameron nodded. "We need to talk. I have something to tell you before we could even think about moving forward."

"Charity's father."

"Yes."

He nodded. "Okay, cool. I'm ready for that. Let's have dinner tonight."

She pulled out of his arms. "My place."

"Sure. Is seven okay?"

She nodded and Gray left the room, but not before he kissed her on the lips. "I love you. Whatever you've got to tell me is going to be okay," he said before he left the room.

Cameron let her body fall into her chair. "It's not going to be okay." She dropped her head back and closed her eyes. She didn't care what he said. It wasn't going to be okay at all.

# Chapter 24

Cameron picked up pizza on her way home, took a hot shower changed into a comfortable pair of knit pants and a top. Jacob had already texted her to let her know he was going to be a few minutes late. Traffic was horrible. It was the Friday before a holiday and people were trying to get out of the city.

He arrived not too long after his text. Cameron served salad and they ate the pizza while they talked about the show.

The Hunter Perry episode had aired the night before and the ratings were through the roof. Jacob wiped his mouth and pushed his plate away from himself. "Advertising for the season run is coming in left and right. It looks like I'll definitely come out of the red on this project. TCT is already talking about a holiday episode, a full season next summer and BET is interested in syndication."

Cameron raised an eyebrow. "Wow! That's amazing."

"You were great. You make this show."

She was so glad he was pleased with her work, even if he wouldn't be that pleased with her soon. Emotion caused her lip to tremble when she spoke. "I'll keep doing my best."

"You are the best," he replied. "You are the perfect person for this role. I knew you would be."

"Hunger is good motivation to perform."

"So is natural talent." Jacob smiled. "We've got a good team too."

She agreed with him but knew her time was winding down. The conversation had lulled. Dinner was finished. It was time to talk.

"It's been a long week," Jacob said. "Can we stretch out on the couch?"

"Sure," she replied standing and taking the dishes into the kitchen. She told him to turn on the television. Cameron cleaned up the kitchen as slowly as a person could possibly do the job. She poked her head through the pass-through and offered him coffee or a soft drink.

"Nope, all I want is to see your pretty face, so come on in here."

She let out a long sigh, said a quick prayer and joined him in the living room. She was terrified. How in the world was she going to tell him about Charity's father? She knew he was probably thinking it was some random guy, but it wasn't. It was the average man's worst nightmare.

Her cell phone rang. Cameron felt like she'd been saved by the bell. "It's my mother. I have to take this." She answered, listened to her mother for a few seconds and her heart froze. "Wait a minute. Mama, what do you mean she's been hit? How? Where is she? Okay, okay, yes, I'm on my way."

Cameron jumped to her feet and Jacob followed. By now, concern was etched on his face. "What is it?"

"My daughter," she cried. "She's been hit by a car."

After a few seconds of a strange kind of silence, they flew into action. Cameron went to her room to pack a few things. Jacob got online to find a flight.

Cameron came out of her bedroom carrying an overnight bag. "What time is the flight?"

Jacob frowned. "It's spring break. All the flights are

booked."

Panic filled every cell in her body. "But that's not possible. I have to get home. They have to operate."

"I know, baby. Just give me a minute. I have an idea." He scrolled though the contacts on the phone and dialed Ethan who picked up on the second ring. "E, I need a huge favor. Cameron's daughter has been in an accident and we need to get to North Carolina. Can you take us?"

"Take us how?" Cameron asked.

Jacob covered the cell phone like it had a mouthpiece. "He's a pilot. He has a plane."

Ethan said yes without hesitation and let them know he needed an hour or so. He had to get on the take-off schedule and submit a flight plan.

Jacob repeated that to Cameron. She merely nodded and then plopped down on the sofa while Gray and Ethan coordinated a few other details.

It wasn't long before they were in the air. The flight was smooth. Gray and Ethan made some small talk in an attempt to break up the quiet in the small aircraft. Listlessly, Cameron stared at the control panel. She tried hard to listen to them because every word of their conversation that she processed helped her to think a little less about what Charity was going through. The travel time was agonizing.

"Did we take you away from Deniece?" she asked, trying to care if the answer was yes when she couldn't fathom him doing anything more important than getting her to North Carolina.

"She had a rehearsal dinner tonight and she has a wedding tomorrow so she already had plans to stay overnight in the Hamptons," he replied. Ethan didn't say anything else. He seemed to sense she needed quiet. So did Jacob. He reached for her hand and squeezed strength into her body. It was then that she realized he was going home with her. She'd been in such a state that she hadn't realized the implications. He was going to meet Charity and if he looked closely, he might know the truth just from looking in her eyes. Gray eyes. There was no denying the honey brown color was unique.

She pulled her hand free from his, dropped her chin on her fist and stared out the window. This accident was tragic in more ways than one, but she couldn't worry about Gray. Not now. The fallout would be what it was going to be. Either he would accept the truth or choose a lie. That was his decision. It was no reflection on her.

Air turbulence caused the plane to bump. Usually a thing like that made her heart race, but it couldn't possibly speed up anymore. Her blood was already in full spin from worry over her daughter and heartache over losing Gray.

# Chapter 25

They arrived at Hickory General after landing at the Asheville airport, renting a car and making the trip east on I-40. Hickory was a few towns over from Kirk. Charity had been taken there because it had better trauma facilities.

They passed a sign that let them know they'd reached the Pediatric Intensive Care Unit. If she hadn't been visiting her own child, Cameron would have thought it was the coolest looking ICU area she'd ever seen. The walls and floors were a cool white color with insets of glass and chrome, so that the rooms and facilities could be viewed from all angles. It was a sexy space that appeared to be brand new. Cameron hoped the care was as top notch as the facility.

There was one woman manning the nurses' station and she was on the phone. Cameron let her eyes do a sweep of the area, in search of her mother. She spotted her in the waiting room. She appeared to be sleeping in a half sitting, half lying position in a corner.

Cameron pointed her out to Gray and Ethan. "I don't want to wake her. "I'm going to look for Charity's room and then see if I can find out what's going on."

They nodded with understanding, but Gray fell into step beside her. A nurse exited a room and offered her assistance.

Cameron responded, "I'm looking for Charity Scott."

Cameron could tell the woman recognized her, but she maintained her professionalism and said, "We just got her settled in her room. She did well in recovery. She's sleeping now. We had to give her something for the discomfort. She's in room five." She pointed and Cameron, followed by Gray, went to the room.

They looked in through the glass door. Cameron gasped at the sight of her daughter. Her head was wrapped in a large bandage. Her arm was in a brace that was suspended in the air. The hand on the other arm was bandaged as well. She folded her body into Grays and shook her head. "My poor baby." All the strength she'd gathered on the trip from the airport seemed to seep from her pores.

Jacob kissed the top of her head. "She's going to be okay. She's here and they're taking good care of her."

Cameron raised her head and looked in his eyes. "Are you sure? How can you be sure? Look at her." She pulled away from him, pushed the door open for the room and approached the bed. The closer she got, the more her heart broke. She reached for Gray's arm. She needed an anchor keep her on her feet. He was an anchor in more ways than one. He whispered words of encouragement and then prayed for Charity. Cameron was glad he was with her. She released the vice grip she had on his arms and took a deep breath. "Thank you for that. I was so emotional I couldn't get my thoughts together."

"She's going to be okay, Cam. I know it. We just have to wait this out."

*We.* The word wasn't lost on her. It implied they were a family and although that warmed her heart, she knew, she and Gray had unfinished business with respect to Charity. She wasn't going to let herself forget what that meant, but she would still draw on his strength. He seemed to have enough of it for both of them.

After about ten minutes, a nurse entered to take some vitals. Cameron asked Jacob to get her mother so she could see Charity. Moments later her mother entered the room. Gray filled the space in the door behind her. Cameron rushed to her mother and wrapped her arms around her. "It's so good to see you, Mama." She choked on sobs.

"I didn't mean to fall asleep. They kept telling me she was on the way up here from surgery and I kept waiting and waiting."

Cameron could feel the intensity of her mother's remorse. She probably felt like she'd fallen asleep on the job completely just because Charity was here. "It's okay. It's the middle of the night. You're not used to being up this late."

Gray placed a hand on her mother's shoulder. "Can I get you a cup of coffee, Ms. Scott?"

Her mother reached up and squeezed his hand. "No, son. I'm not much of a coffee drinker. I'll be okay."

Cameron's eyes connected with his and she felt so drawn to him that she was almost embarrassed to admit it to herself. It was impossible to appreciate him more than she did at this very moment. He had taken complete control from the moment she found out Charity was hurt. She would be forever grateful to him.

Gray seemed to sense the focus of her thoughts had shifted to him, because he gave her a warm smile. He let go of her mother's hand, took a few steps toward her and took her hands in his. "What about you? Do you want some coffee or something?"

She shook her head. "I have everything I need right here in this room."

He smiled again, pulled her into an embrace and whispered, "I'm going to let you two have some time together. I'll go wait with Ethan."

He made his exit and Cameron returned her attention to Charity. She thought about Gray's prayers and declaration of healing and said, "Our little girl is going to be okay, Mama."

They took seats and wordlessly stared at Charity for a long time before her mother stated, "Jacob looks good."

Cameron nodded.

"What's he doing here?"

"He and I were together when I found out."

"I know that, but that's not a reason to get on a plane with somebody."

Cameron shook her head and closed her eyes. "I don't want to talk about Jacob right now."

"You never want to talk about Jacob. That's part of ya problem," her mother said. Cameron rolled her eyes and groaned inwardly. This was not the time, but she knew her mother didn't care. "He still looks at you the way he did when you two first got married. That man loves you. After all these years, he still loves you."

Cameron raised her eyes to her mothers. "I want to focus on Charity."

"I'm thinking about Charity," her mother replied. "I'm thinking about both of you."

Cameron knew where her mother was going with this. It was always about a man with her mother. Nothing in life was good enough unless it had a man attached to it.

They were quiet for a few more minutes, both slipped into solemn states. Her mother began to cry. She reached into her handbag for a tissue and swiped under her eyes before speaking. "I let her get off the bus by herself. She's only been doing it for two weeks. I watch from the porch every day, but the car came from nowhere. It was moving so fast."

"Mama, it's not your fault. It was an accident. She's

going to recover."

"Her little arm was just about crushed," her mother cried some more. Cameron was out of her seat and at her mother's side in an instant. She rubbed her mother's back when she spoke. " Mama, it's almost two in the morning. You're tired. There's no point in all of us sleeping here. Let me stay. You go home with Grandma. She's probably worried and you know that's not good for her heart."

Her mother nodded. "I hate to leave before she wakes up, but I do need to see about Mama."

The two women re-joined Ethan and Jacob in the waiting room.

"My mom needs to go home."

Ethan stood and said, "I can take you, ma'am."

Cameron picked up her mother's coat and helped her into it. "Mama, is it all right if Ethan stays at the house? He'll be heading back to New York in the morning."

"Of course," her mother replied. "I can't thank you enough for bringing Cameron home."

Cameron wrapped her arms around Ethan's neck and thanked him for everything.

"No, problem. Just let me know if you need anything else," he said.

He and Gray exchanged a few words. Cameron's mother gathered her handbag and walked out with him.

Cameron released a breath and closed her eyes. When she opened them she gave Gray a weak smile. They went back to Charity's room. He sat down and pulled her onto to his lap.

"Are you sure you don't want to go to the house? You'll be uncomfortable in these chairs."

Gray shook his head. "There's absolutely nothing on earth that could pull me away from you right now." He raised a finger and swept her hair back off her forehead.

She appreciated him being here. The truth was she didn't really want to be alone and his words were so reassuring. She needed his strength. "I don't know how to thank you."

"You don't have to thank me. I love you. Haven't you figured it out yet? I'll do anything for you."

Cameron closed her eyes tight and folded her body into his arms. "We still have to talk," she whispered.

"When Charity's better," Gray replied.

She dropped her head onto his shoulder. "Yes, when she's better."

# Chapter 26

The next day was a long and miserable. Charity was in a lot of pain so the hospital staff kept her medicated and the medication made her sleep. Jacob watched as Cameron suffered through the agony of watching her child wrestle with pain.

By the second day, Charity was somewhat better and Jacob was relieved, not only for the little girl, but for Cameron. She kept up a strong, brave front, but it was obvious her daughter's pain was hurting her more than it might have even been hurting Charity.

He checked into a hotel room across the street so they could shower, change and grab short naps. Cameron's mother, relatives, friends and church members visited as well. During those times he didn't feel bad about leaving Cameron, so he was able to go back to the room and get some work done. He wished Cameron would join him and at least get more than two hours of sleep, but she was not leaving Charity's side.

"You can go back to New York," she offered. "I appreciate what you've done for us, but you don't have to stay here. I know you have work to do."

Jacob let out a deep breath. "I'm not leaving you. I'm not being polite."

Cameron sat back in her seat and rotated her coffee cup between her hands. He couldn't read her. The timing was too bad to push the relationship conversation, but he wanted her to know he wasn't going away.

"You're so close to home. I'm surprised you don't have friends you want to visit while you're here," she said.

"Or my family," he replied. "I should want to see them."

Cameron made a strange noise and her voice was tight when she spoke. "I forget how many relatives you have."

"Too many on my mom's side."

Cameron avoided his eyes.

He reached for her hand, which had abandoned the coffee cup and was now balled in a fist on the table. "We don't have as many on my dad's side. He was an only child and quite a few of his cousins didn't have children. I'm the last of the Gray males. It feels weird to know that when it started out being my brother and I. I remember him saying his wife would have to have at least three boys so he could be sure the name wouldn't die out. It's sad to think he didn't have any."

She yanked her hand free and pushed her chair back. "I'm sorry, I can't ..." She stood. "I'm not in the mood to talk about your brother or your family right now." She shook her head. She wanted to ask for forgiveness for being so abrupt, but she couldn't even do that. "I'm going back to Charity's room."

\*\*\*

Jacob had a sick feeling in the pit of his stomach. *His brother. His family.* She'd had this strange reaction a few weeks ago and he'd forgotten to get to the bottom of it. He was perplexed. Cameron barely knew his family. He'd taken her to meet his parents and Justin the weekend after they'd eloped. The only other time she spent time with them was during the family reunion. His father was…well, his father. He specialized in making him feel bad. Now, he wondered how much nastier he might have been to Cameron?

He cursed under his breath. He had subjected her to some Gray drama and hadn't even known it. Instinctively, he knew whatever it was had been damaging, because the hairs on the back of his neck were standing up. That rarely happened to him, but every time it did, he knew God was making him uncomfortable, so he would pay attention. He reached into his pocket for his cell phone and dialed a number that he hadn't called in nearly a year.

"Gray residence." Jacob recognized the voice of Henry, the butler. Henry had been with the family for nearly fifteen years, arriving shortly after the death of the man who had worked for the Gray family for nearly forty years.

"Henry, this is Jacob. How are you?"

"Master Jacob, I'm well." Jacob could tell by his tone he was glad to hear his voice. "I gather since you called on the house phone and not my cell phone that you want to speak to your father."

"Yes, sir, I do. Is he there?"

"He's gone out on his boat, but he did tell me to expect him for dinner."

"Good, add another setting to the table. I'll be there as well."

There was silence on the other end of the phone. Jacob hadn't been home since his brother passed three years earlier and prior to that, it was his mother's death the year before that. He'd thought about that pattern, but hadn't done a thing to make things right between himself and his father. They definitely needed help in the fixing department. Their relationship was a little more than strained. It had been strained his entire life. His older brother, Justin, had been his father's favorite child. As a result, his father had spoiled Justin. By the time he realized what a mess he'd made of the young man, it was too late. Justin was getting into all kinds of trouble and in general failing to live up to any kind of responsibility. Justin would have run the family business, for which his father had tried to groom him, into the ground.

After his death, his father's half-hearted suggestions that Jacob run Gray Building and Construction Company were rejected by him for several reasons; one, he had no intention of pinch hitting for his deceased brother and two, his love was film. He wouldn't give that up to satisfy anyone, including his father.

"I'm driving from Hickory, so I'll be almost three hours."

"And how long are you staying, Sir?"

"Just overnight."

"Are you alone or do you have a companion?"

"I'm alone."

"Fine, then. I'll prepare your room and add a setting to the table. It will be good to see you, Sir."

They ended the call and Jacob returned to Charity's room. Cameron's eyes were closed. She was praying again. He hated to leave her, but he needed some answers. He didn't want to interrupt her so he opted to call her once he got on the road.

When he told her he was going home for the afternoon, she responded with a simple, "okay" and told him to have a safe trip, but her tone was odd, again. He didn't question her. She was under enough stress. He was also sure answers were waiting at the end of his trip.

\*\*\*

Jacob beat his father home and spent the afternoon talking to Henry and Helen. Helen was Henry's wife. She had also been the maid/cook/unofficial nanny that his father's parents had employed. She'd been with the family for nearly forty years. As far as Jacob knew, his father was in the house alone. He couldn't imagine that his dad actually needed Henry now. He probably never had, but he supposed it was easier to have someone supervise the staff that gardened, kept up the pool and did the maintenance on the twenty acres. Plus, his father had the money.

"I think I'm going to retire next year," Mrs. Helen said, picking up their empty lemonade glasses and putting them in the dishwasher.

Jacob huffed. "You can't. You're too young and my father would be lost without you."

"I'm sixty five and I'm tired. These young gals I get in here are making my blood pressure go up. None of 'em can clean. If your mother were alive she'd skin all of 'em."

Jacob laughed. "Mrs. Helen, you know they don't make women like you or my mother anymore."

Mrs. Helen perched a hand on her hip. "So is that why you haven't had one? I thought that wife of yours was a nice young lady. I see you two are working together. Second chances can be a good thing."

Jacob smiled agreeably. "I came to North Carolina with her. She's in Hickory. Her daughter's in the hospital."

"Daughter?" Helen was confused. "I didn't know Ms. Cameron had a child."

"A five year-old."

Mrs. Helen shook her head. "Five years old and she's not –?" She stopped herself.

Jacob answered the unasked question. "No ma'am. I know I never told you or my family why I left Cameron, but it was because of that pregnancy."

Mrs. Helen was silent for a moment. "Is the child okay?"

"Yes, she was hit by a car and had to have surgery. She's out of the woods for the most part but still in ICU and heavily drugged."

Mrs. Helen nodded. "I'll add her to my prayer list."

"We would appreciate that."

Mrs. Helen seemed oddly pensive. Just when he was about to ask her what was on her mind she spoke. "If you don't mind my asking, how did you and Ms. Cameron get back together? It's been so many years. "

"The stories in the media are true. I came back to the U.S. for her. I hired her because she was out of work."

"So what you really mean is you wanted your wife back?" Henry's laughter filled the kitchen.

Jacob smiled. "Yes, sir. I didn't give her a chance to explain herself years ago. Not that it would have mattered back then, but still we didn't have any closure."

"Maybe it would have mattered," Mrs. Helen offered.

Jacob sighed loudly. "I have a feeling there's something I don't know. That's why I'm here. I need to talk to my father."

Jacob didn't miss the way she'd cut her eyes to Henry or the strained look on her face.

"Mrs. Helen, you were here during the family reunion. I know it was a long time ago, but do you remember anything that happened that weekend? To Cameron, I mean. Was anyone rude? Did she seem uncomfortable?"

Mrs. Helen's eyebrows knit a wary line. "Mr. Jacob, I think you best talk to your father."

Jacob leaned back in his chair. He knew this woman. Whenever her shoulders got tight and her forehead got wrinkled it was a sign that she was holding something back, but before he could push Henry rescued her.

"Helen, we should set the table for dinner. Master Jacob, your father just pulled his truck into the outer garage."

Mrs. Helen gave him one last pensive look and left the room with her husband. Irked, Jacob slapped a palm on the table. Something had happened. He wanted to kick himself for letting all these years get between him and the truth. What did everyone know that he didn't?

Determined to find out, he stood and left the house by the backdoor to take the short walk to his father's work shed. He refused to let anger build on the walk. He knew his father. Words expressed in anger were a sure way to shut the man down. Although she'd rarely used them, his mother's sharp tone was the only one he heeded.

Jacob hesitated before going in. He hadn't seen his father in years and was only here now because he was on a mission to get information. He felt a little guilty about that, but then remembered why he didn't come home and didn't call. They didn't like each other. His father had no respect for him and Jacob was sick of his contempt. He squared his shoulders, turned the doorknob and walked in. He didn't expect to see what he found.

His father was older; much older looking than Jacob ever imagined he'd see him. He'd never been a heavy man, but now he was thin, down at least thirty pounds. Most of his hair was gone and what was left was completely white. Losing his mother and son must have been a heavier burden on his heart than Jacob realized.

The door creaked and his father turned toward the sound. He blinked a few times like he needed to be sure of what he was seeing. "My God. Jacob."

"Dad."

Jacob did a visual sweep of the room. His father was a man with many hobbies. Boating, fishing, golf and tennis, but his favorite of them all had always been building models. When Jacob was a small child, his father worked on model cars and airplanes. As he grew, so did his father's models until he'd moved on to building airports and small towns. Now, it appeared he was working on a model of an entire city. His father took a few steps to close the distance between them. "Why didn't you tell me you were coming?"

"I made the decision just this morning."

His father studied him for a moment. "You look well."

Jacob stuck his hands in his pockets and nodded.

"You can't say the same for me," his father chuckled. "Don't worry. I feel worse than I look. I feel a hundred."

Guilt ripped through him. He'd been such an absentee son he didn't feel he had a right to ask, but he did anyway. "How's your health?"

His father sighed. His eyes roamed the room. He walked back over to where he'd been standing and opened a small wooden box on the table. He removed a figurine, held it up to the overhead light and said, "I see you have a television show in the United States. It's nice you're home."

"It's good to be home. New York has taken some getting used to, but it's not much different from London."

His father raised his eyes, gave him a look that Jacob wasn't sure how to read. "I also see you're working with Cameron and you've had Hunter Perry on the show."

"I'm surprised you took an interest."

His father frowned. "You're my child, Jacob. Why wouldn't I be interested?"

Jacob didn't respond to that. It had only been five minutes. He didn't want to fight. His father removed a label from the figurine's bottom and placed it on a shelf with a few others. Jacob approached the table. "So, this is Raleigh. I recognize the Municipal Rose Garden."

"You know how your mother loved that garden."

Jacob's heart smiled.

"If they would have let me, I would have buried her there."

"I rode past the family plot when I came in. There are more than enough roses to keep her happy."

His father grunted. "I don't know. There never seemed to be enough roses for that woman." He tossed the empty box into a nearby trash receptacle. "How long are you staying?"

"Just tonight."

"You have an agenda?"

"I have some questions."

His father pitched an eyebrow. "About your trust fund?"

Jacob shook his head. "Of course not. Why would you think that?"

His father shrugged. "You hadn't accessed it. I thought you might want to begin to draw from it."

"I'm not here about money, Dad."

"Good. I'm glad to know you don't need any." His father moved a few more pieces around. One was a tall lithe African-American woman dressed in a gray suit. He placed it at the entrance to the high school. Jacob realized it was a model of a school teacher. He also realized it was likely his mother. She'd been a teacher in the early years of their marriage.

His father surveyed his work. "You know I never talk on an empty stomach. Let's go up to the house and have dinner."

\*\*\*

Henry served one of Jacob's favorite meals, which included fried chicken, macaroni and cheese, collard greens and cornbread. His father was served baked fish and a salad, but he partook of Mrs. Helen's irresistible cornbread.

Once they'd eaten, Jacob got to the point of his visit. "Dad, Cameron did something yesterday that made me think that something happened to her years ago, during the family reunion."

"You mean the last one you missed before you missed the last five?"

His father's effort to infuse sarcasm into his tone was successful.

"Yes, that one. The one that was a few months after my wedding."

His father sat back in his chair, tossed his napkin in his plate and said, "You didn't have a wedding. You ran off to Charleston like you didn't have any family, class, or money and you got married by a judge."

Jacob swallowed. "I got married the way I wanted to."

His father grunted. "The way you started did wonders for the marriage, didn't it?"

Jacob shook his head. *Here we go*, he thought.

"I don't care what you decided. You stole that wedding from your mother and it broke her heart."

Jacob swallowed guilt. "I didn't think about that. I never anticipated she would get sick…" he paused. "I was thinking with my heart. I was in love. I'm… still in love." Jacob paused. "Anyway, I'm not here to discuss what I did. I can't undo it. I just want to know if you remember anything happening to Cameron during that weekend."

His father groaned. "You see her every day, don't you? It seems you would ask her that."

"I'm asking you."

"What makes you think something happened?"

"I don't know. It was something she said."

"And that was?"

"She behaved like I'd put a spider down her blouse when I mentioned our family."

His father reached for his water goblet and took a long sip. "Did you ask her why?"

"No, it's a long story, but I didn't get the chance. That's why I'm here."

His father put down his glass and stood. He looked nervous, sick. "I need some air," he said. "Let's go on the deck."

Jacob wasn't crazy. His father was moving from place to place; dodging the question like the professional he was, professional at controlling a dialogue and being evasive.

They went out on the deck. His father lit a cigar. In the thirty years they'd owned this house, his father had never smoked inside. His mother forbade it.

"Still smoking outside," Jacob said stepping closer to his father.

"Some habits die hard. Besides, if I lit up in the house your mother would haunt me."

Jacob laughed. "She would try her best."

"It'd be good to see her. Even if she was a ghost." His father's eyelid twitched when he said that. "I miss her. I can't tell you how it feels to miss a woman after living and loving her for over thirty years."

"I think I can imagine what that's like. I tried to get over Cameron. I've been seven thousand miles away and it still felt like she had her hand in my chest squeezing my heart." Jacob sighed. "Everything isn't peachy like it says in the media. We've got some things to work through, but I'm determined to fix it. My gut is telling me I need your help."

His father was quiet for a long time. Long enough to smoke his cigar down halfway. Reading his face was like watching a movie. The expressions went from tense and angry to curious and fearful. Finally he spoke. "Why did you leave her, son? What happened?"

"I found out she'd done something and I thought it was unforgiveable."

His father was quiet again.

"Dad, I'm going to tell you the truth. I've kept it to myself for years, but I'm here without announcement. I at least owe you something." He swallowed his pride and continued. "Cameron cheated on me. She was pregnant, almost three months when I found out."

His father walked to a table and stubbed the cigar out.

"I found her ultrasound. I knew based on the dates that it couldn't be my baby, because I was in Africa."

His father frowned and a hundred worry lines exploded on his face. "What did she have to say for herself?"

"She didn't have anything to say. I mean she kept

175

saying I didn't understand and asking me to listen to her, but I didn't want to know about the guy. I didn't want to know the details. I packed my stuff and left."

His father's expression was curious. "Where is the child?"

"Her daughter is the reason I'm in North Carolina. She was in a car accident—,"

"Daughter?" The thinned jowls below his father's chin moved with his Adam's apple. He instantly paled and raised a hand to his chest. "Do me a favor. Get my pills out of the top pocket of the jacket I was wearing."

Jacob dashed back into the house, found the jacket on the back of his father's favorite chair. He looked at the bottle. It was heart medication. He ran back out on the deck and handed the open bottle to his father. "You're taking heart medication? Since when?" Jacob went to the small bar area and poured a glass of water handing it to his father as well.

His father tossed the pill into his mouth and followed it with a long sip. Then he took a seat. "I had a minor heart attack shortly after your brother passed. I've been on these pills ever since."

"Why didn't you tell me?"

"I haven't talked to you. You've been gone trying to forget Cameron and apparently trying to forget me. And there's no point badgering Henry about it. I made him swear on his job not to tell you. If my own son can't call *me* to find out how I'm doing then he doesn't deserve to know." His father closed the pill bottle and put it in his shirt pocket. "I need to rest, son." He stood. "Can we talk more in the morning?"

Jacob was dying for answers, but one more night of waiting wouldn't kill him. Badgering his father might finish him off. "Of course. I'm leaving pretty early, but I know you're an early riser so we'll talk over breakfast."

"That we will," his father said. He put a hand on Jacob's shoulder, looked reflectively into his eyes and smiled a little. "I'll see you in the morning."

"I'll check on you in a few."

His father shook his head. "Not necessary. I'm usually alone and I have one of these." He raised his wrist and Jacob noted his father's watch was a lifeline signaling device. "Henry and Helen take care of me."

Jacob watched his father walk back into the house. From his view, he could see him take the elevator rather than the stairs. Jacob sighed hard and heavy, but he also thanked God for Henry and Helen.

He reentered the house, plopped down on a sofa and closed his eyes. He thought about his loved ones. His brother had committed suicide. His father had suffered a heart attack he didn't know about. Cameron had had years of problems that almost led to alcoholism. He'd thought so much of himself when he was overseas making a name for himself in the indie film industry. Now he realized he had been a coward. He'd run away from everyone who meant something to him. All relationships were for better or worse. As a grown man, he should have been able to better manage the ones in his circle. The first step in doing that would have been to simply stay in touch.

Upon that realization, he removed his cell phone from his pocket and placed a call to Cameron.

"How's Charity?" he asked when her voice came on the line.

He could hear her sigh. "She's in and out of it. I think the anesthesia really affected her. I know she's on pain medication, but she's so sleepy. She's hardly been awake."

"Her body is resting. It's good for her to sleep. She has a concussion, a broken arm, a dislocated shoulder and all that bruising."

"It's only by God's grace that she's alive," Cameron cried. "I just want to see her eyes. I want her to look at me, so I can know she's okay."

"You'll see them soon. I know you will. Just hold on." Jacob prayed his words were true, because his heart was breaking for her. "I hate I had to leave you."

He heard her sigh again. "How's your father?" Her tone was clipped, more evidence that he was in the right place.

"His health isn't good. Apparently, he had a heart attack a few years ago. He needed to rest, so we only spoke briefly."

"You didn't know about the heart attack?"

Shamed swallowed him. "No. Trust me, I know how messed up that is, but I've been doing some soul searching. Cutting him off the way I did was selfish."

"You were angry with him."

"More like tired of him being disappointed in me. That get's old, but he's still my father."

Cameron was quiet for a beat. "You're being too hard on yourself."

"I could be. He wasn't easy on me. Sometimes he cut me to the bone."

"I believe that." There was more curtness and then another long pause. "I miss you. When will you be back?"

Jacob's eyes closed. He smiled inwardly. She missed him. "In the morning. Right after my father and I have breakfast, so no later than ten or eleven."

"Good," she said. "It looks like Charity is moving in

there, so I'm going to go back in the room."

"Give her a kiss for me, okay."

More of that silence that spoke volumes of uncertainty took up a moment of their time.

"Cam, I really am looking forward to getting to know her. I'm not just saying that."

"One day at a time. First she has to get better."

"Right."

"Have a good night and drive safe in the morning."

"I'll text you when I'm on the way," he replied and although he was worn out from the drive he offered, "Don't hesitate to call me later if you want to talk."

"I won't," she said. "Goodnight, Gray."

They ended the call. He went into the kitchen to seek out Helen and Henry. He would try to get something out of Helen, but he knew it was likely all she'd give him was more of her cornbread.

# Chapter 27

All that praying and begging God had worked. Charity opened her eyes and for the first time in days she seemed to have completely come out of the hazy state she'd been in. Cameron stroked her cheek. "Hey Ladybug."

"Mommy," Charity whispered. "I was scared I wasn't going to see you anymore."

Cameron shook her head and reached down and gave her daughter the best squeeze she could give her without disturbing her arm or shoulder. Charity tried to hug her back. She soaked in the child's warmth and sweetness, thinking her heart would explode with love.

"Mommy is sorry it's been so long since I was home."

"It's okay. Nan said your work is like those soldiers that have to go away from their kids. Being away is how they work."

Tears filled Cameron's eyes. How easy it was for a child to forgive. How accepting they were of some things that should not be acceptable. She didn't want to take anything away from her mother's kind explanation, so she nodded in agreement and said, "It's kinda the same, isn't it?" But it wasn't. Soldiers were deployed. They had important missions that took them away. She chose to leave her little girl, because she wanted a career that had nothing to do with duty. Or was it even about her career?

Cameron had had nearly three painful days of watching her child sleep to think about her choices, about how easy it had been to make them and why. Deep down in her heart she knew, the pregnancy had cost her. No matter how much she tried to bury the memory of Justin violating her, the pregnancy, the birth and the child were tangible proof of what had happened to her. She loved her daughter, but she resented her at the same time. She hadn't really digested that, until she almost lost her.

"Is Nana here?" Charity asked.

"She was, but she went home to see about Great-Nan."

"I was gonna go to the horse show today," Charity said, sadly.

Realizing the child had lost days, Cameron replied, "I think that was yesterday. But when you get better, I promise I'll find a horse show for us to go to."

"Really, Mommy, me and you?" Charity's entire face lit up. Cameron's heart sank. Her daughter was surprised she would do something as simple as take her to a horse show. She could hear it in her tone. Sure, she'd taken her out when she came home…to the movies, shopping, fancy dinners, to get mani-pedis and to the hair salon, but Cameron had no idea Charity even liked horses. Her trips home hadn't been what they should have been. They'd been about her and what she thought Charity wanted. Not her child. If the Emmy Award could go to the worst mother, Cameron had a feeling she'd win hands down.

Charity began to cough. Cameron poured a cup of water and held it for her to drink. Once her throat was clear, she pulled the chair closer to Charity's bed and sat. She laid a hand on the child's belly and asked, "What else do you like besides horses, baby?"

Charity gave her a long list from Mickey Mouse to Transformers to boats and Cameron knew what she'd be doing this summer. She'd be making up lost affection and lost time with her daughter. She was so glad she had a second chance to make it all right.

\*\*\*

Light peeked in from the window. Cameron rose from the makeshift bed in the corner of Charity's room to find a shadowy figure standing in the doorway. She stretched and careened her neck to see who it was.

"I'm sorry," the man said stepping into the room. "I didn't mean to wake you."

Her mouth fell open. David Gray. Fear clenched her heart. It stopped beating for just a moment. "What are you doing here? Did something happen to Jacob?"

"Jacob is on his way. I think I've got him beat by an hour, but his fury at waking to find me gone is probably better fuel than the gasoline in his car."

Cameron reached into her pocket for her cell phone. She'd had it on mute for the night. She swiped the screen and noted three missed calls and two text messages from Jacob this morning.

"I'm sure Jacob has called you, but please let me speak to you before you call him back."

Cameron shook her head and whispered. "Why are you here?"

"I had to come. I had to see you and I needed to see her," he said casting a glance at Charity's sleeping figure. He took a few steps closer and stared down.

Cameron joined him from the opposite side of the bed.

"Why didn't you tell me about her?" he asked. "When you came to the house that day."

"I wasn't there to see you. I was looking for Jacob."

"But if you had told me."

"What? Was it going to mean something to you? I wasn't taking that chance. You'd already let me know how you dealt with secrets."

He shook his head. "Cameron, I made a mistake, but I had a right to know about her. I would have had those years…" he paused. "Don't you think I had the right?"

Cameron felt her anger rising. "Let's step out."

She went to the door and held it open, but David Gray continued to stand by the bedside staring at Charity. She'd never seen such a tender look in his eyes and when he finally pulled himself away from her, they were filled with unshed tears. He stepped into the corridor.

"I always wanted a little girl in my life," he said attempting to smile, but the rueful look on his face betrayed him. It had only been four years since she'd seen him last, but he looked so old. He was so thin, like he'd aged to a hundred. Cameron knew he was only in his late fifties. Jacob said he had been sick, but that wasn't all of it. Those tears told the story of a man with regrets.

They took the few steps across the corridor and entered the small waiting room, which, fortunately for them, was empty. Mr. Gray sat down.

"Would you like a cup of coffee? They have some in the break room next door."

He shook his head. "No, I gave it up a few years ago. Caffeine makes my heart race."

Cameron sat across from him.

"You look well," he stated.

She didn't reply. She didn't know what to say about that. He'd never seemed to be impressed with any aspect of her before.

"My son will be here soon, so I need to get right to the

point. I owe you an apology."

"An apology?" She shook her head. "I never thought I'd get that. I'm not sure I even want it at this point."

"But I have to give it you if I'm going to make this right."

"You think you can make this right?"

"I can try."

Cameron swallowed and shook her head again.

"I'm sorry about how I treated you."

"It seems you're sorry because of her."

"That's not all of it."

"The last time I saw you, you treated me like dirt. You wouldn't even let me into the foyer of your home. Now you want to apologize because you have a grandchild. You thought it was okay to treat me the way you did when you didn't know she existed."

"No, it wasn't. I handled things poorly. My wife was at death's door. I didn't want her to be any sicker than she already was. If she found out what Justin did it would have killed her."

Cameron let out a long sigh, stood and folded her arms over her chest. "She didn't have to know."

"Of course she would have had to know. If I had known about the child, I would have had to tell her." He paused, a tear spilled onto his cheek. He raised a hand to wipe it. "I would have had to tell her everything." He removed two envelopes from his jacket pocket and handed one to Cameron.

"I should have tried to get that to you. I realize now that I betrayed my Justin's wishes by not doing so, but I pushed it out of my mind. I thought, she's gone from our lives, so what does it matter? And then you came back into Jacob's life and I knew I had to deal with it. I've been ashamed for so many years that it was hard to pull myself out of my shame." He paused. David Gray seemed reflective for a long time before speaking again. "My son came to me yesterday. He told me how much he loves you. That he wants to make a life with you. I knew I had to be honest with him, but before I could be honest with him, I had to be honest with myself and I had to talk to you."

Cameron's eyes filled with tears. She wished this conversation didn't mean so much to her. "Justin raped me, you threatened me and then Jacob left me. Both of them broke my heart. Both of them treated me like a whore. Is that what you taught them? That simple little country girls like me are just disposable?"

He shook his head. "I don't know. I'd be lying if I didn't say I gave them the impression that they were supposed to marry a woman with a similar background."

Cameron pitched an eyebrow, "Impression?"

"Okay, directive. I thought those things mattered. I never wanted a woman to use them for their money."

"And girls with good breeding aren't looking for money?"

He lowered his eyes. "I guess I thought they were more worthy."

Cameron frowned at his admission, but she couldn't say she didn't already know that's what he thought. He'd made it clear years ago that he didn't think she was good enough for his son.

"I told you I was being honest. I haven't always been a good person, but now, the older I get the more I realize how wrong I was. I'm sorry for the pain I caused you."

"Sorry? Your sons destroyed my life and you helped

them."

He reached for her hand, the one that she'd just used to wipe her tears. Another tear of his own slid down his cheek. "I'm sorry I treated you badly. I'm sorry I didn't make Justin pay for what he did. If I had been a better man, I would have made him own up to what he did before his brother, his mother, the law and God. That is the biggest mistake I have ever made in my life. Not making that boy pay."

Cameron closed her eyes. She searched her heart for more angry words, but couldn't find any. She wished he wasn't being so sincere. She wanted to continue to resent him, but his eyes, his slumped shoulders, his white hair and his mad dash down the interstate to meet her told the story. He was not someone who could be hated anymore. Not by her. She slid back against her chair and used her fingers to wipe the tears away.

He reached into the pocket of his blazer and removed a handkerchief. Even though he needed it himself, he handed it to her. "I can't take back what I did, but I swear to heaven, if you'll let me, I'll never ever hurt my granddaughter. I'll be the best grandfather any little girl could ever have."

Cameron pulled her hand from his. *Grandfather,* she thought. He wanted to stake some claim on her Charity. After all these years he wanted some ownership. That didn't seem fair.

"I don't know about letting you into our lives like that."

He cast his eyes down again and then raised them. "You can't change who I am, Cameron. Being angry with me doesn't change what I am to her."

Cameron let the word, grandfather swirl around in her head for a few minutes. A grandfather was something she'd never had. Like herself, Charity didn't have a single man in her life. If Cameron didn't do anything about that, she'd grow up in a manless world just like she had. She'd be another statistic. She'd be another little black girl with no father, no grandfather, no uncles or men to show her what it was like to be loved by a man who wasn't trying to date or bed her. She wanted better for her daughter. She'd prayed about it for years. But could it be this man? This man who'd hurt her so much.

She looked into David Gray's eyes. Searched them for his truth. Would he be the man who would tell Charity she was beautiful? Would he sit and allow her to play tea party with him? Would he take walks with her and read books with her? Was it possible, that David Gray would do those things she so ached and wished she'd had a father or grandfather to do when she was a child?

His eyes said yes. His eyes said he was old and lonely. His eyes said he needed love, and she heard them. She heard every word they transferred from his spirit to hers.

"I don't know if I can trust you, but I know if I was my daughter, I'd want me to try." She slipped her hand back into his and squeezed it. "Your granddaughter's name is Charity Renee Scott."

David Gray smiled. His chest heaved up and down releasing sobs of relief. At that moment, Cameron thought choosing forgiveness had been the right decision.

# Chapter 28

Jacob pulled into the hospital parking lot. As the note had said, his father would be here. What was foremost on his mind was the question he'd been asking himself for hours… what business did his father have with Cameron? Why would he get up before five a.m. and drive nearly three hours to come to this hospital?

He entered the building, stepped into the elevator and pushed the button. Fortunately, pediatrics was on the second floor, so it took less than a minute for him to reach the floor and make the short trip to Charity's room.

Charity was sitting up watching television. Jacob was astounded by the transformation to the sleepy little girl he'd been looking at every day. If it hadn't been for the bandage on her head and the cast on her arm, he'd have never known she was in such a horrific accident.

He approached the bed. "Hi, Charity. I'm Jacob. I'm a friend of your moms."

She looked at him strangely. It was an assessment a grown woman would make. It made him laugh inwardly. She seemed satisfied that he was okay to talk to. "You're my mommy's boss, aren't you?"

He smiled. "Yes, I am her boss, but I'm also a good friend. How are you feeling this morning?"

"My head doesn't hurt anymore."

"That's good. I'm glad to hear that." Jacob felt awkward. He'd never spent much time around kids. He wished he was a natural like Ethan. At this very moment, he needed some of his friend's finesse in the kiddo small talk department, but Charity didn't seem interested in him. Her eyes were glued to the television. He looked up at the program and asked, "What are you watching?"

She giggled. "Penguins of Madagascar."

Jacob walked closer to the bed and took a seat next to her. "Madagascar," he replied. "Really? Do you know where Madagascar is?"

She turned those big brown eyes on him and shook her head no. Now that her eyes were open and the bandage under her chin was removed, she looked oddly familiar. It was her eyes that seemed like eyes he'd looked into a million times, but she didn't really look like Cameron. Not at all.

"Madagascar is an island off the coast of southeast Africa," he said. "Do you know what Africa is?"

"It's a continent," she replied picking up a carton of milk and taking a sip.

He was impressed that a five year old knew Africa was a continent.

"Well, I've been to Madagascar."

She snatched her head back. If she was old enough to remember the old sitcom she would have asked, "What you talkin' about Willis?" Instead, her lips released a gasp. "For real?"

"For real. I filmed a documentary there."

"What's a doc-a-mentary?"

"A documentary is a movie or a film about real life stuff."

Her eyes grew to the size of saucers. "Did you see any Penguins?"

"No. I'm pretty sure Penguins don't actually live in Madagascar."

She twisted up her lips. "Well, they're lost on the show anyway. They're from the New York Zoo."

"That explains it," he replied.

Charity picked up her milk again and winced when she did so. All her hospital tubing was in her left arm and the child was apparently left-handed because she was naturally attempting to use it.

"I have an idea. How about I hold the milk for you?" Jacob took the carton from her hand.

Charity nodded and allowed him to do so. "Nana said you been knowing my mommy for a long time."

"Yeah, I've known her before you were born."

"You like her."

"Yes, I do, but how do you know that?"

"I saw you on the T.V. with Mommy and you looked at her like you want to marry her."

Jacob put the carton down. She was a perceptive little woman that was for sure. "Do you think your mommy should get married?"

"I don't know. I guess. She's pretty enough to get married. She's pretty like my Bride Barbie."

"Yes," Jacob agreed. "Your mother is definitely beautiful."

"Can I have some more milk please?"

She looked at him intensely and once again he felt that familiar feeling about her. It was comfortable and uncomfortable at the same time. He liked feeling at ease with her, but he thought it was eerie to feel so strongly that he'd seen her before.

Jacob picked up the carton. When he did so, the girl put her hand on the outside of his as she took a sip. He looked at her tiny little hand and thought about how easy it seemed to fit on his. How complicated life had gotten because this little girl whom was so easy to talk to had been growing in her mother's belly. He looked down at the name bracelet and noted her last name was Scott. He looked at more of the information, birth date, age and then noted the blood typing tag on the bracelet. She was AB negative.

He returned the carton to the tray. Just then his father walked into the room. At that moment, Jacob realized why Charity's eyes looked so familiar. He looked from her to his father and thought about his own image. Those eyes were Gray eyes.

"You got here fast," his father spoke like they weren't about to have the nastiest fight of their lives. "Did you get a speeding ticket?"

Jacob didn't respond. His father walked around to the other side of the bed, opened a small container of yogurt he'd been carrying and placed it on Charity's breakfast tray.

"Here you go," he said in a voice that Jacob had never in his life heard. It was saccharine sweet, loving and adoring, all very unlike his father.

"Thank you, Mr. Gray," Charity replied reaching for the spoon his father had stuck in the container.

Unable to sit any longer, Jacob stood. "Where's Cameron?"

His father was so engaged in a conversation with Charity that he seemed to have completely tuned him out.

"Dad," he said firmly. "Where is Cameron?"

His father stood upright. "She's in the restroom, I believe."

"Can we talk outside?"

"Sure." He met Jacob's eyes, swallowed and said, "Charity, I'll be back in a few minutes." They stepped out into the hall and his father said, "I'm sorry I left like that. I know I owe you an explanation."

Jacob shook his head. "I'm not even believing you right this moment. Did you say you owe me an explanation? What is going on?"

"It's complicated. We need to sit down and talk about it, but the corridor isn't the place to do it." His father took a few steps, opened the waiting room door, peeked in and pulled it closed. "There are people in there," he said, nervously.

*Nervous.* Jacob didn't think he'd ever seen his father look this scared, not even when his mother was sick. Who was this man in the hallway outside of Cameron's daughter's room looking so very different from the controlled man he'd grown up with?

"That little girl is a Gray and we both know she isn't mine." Jacob spoke through clenched teeth. "Is she your daughter?"

Adamantly, he shook his head. "Of course not. What kind of question is that?"

"It's a question that needs to be asked." Jacob stuck his hands in his pockets. He paced a few times before he spoke. "Then that only leaves one other explanation, she has our blood type and our eyes. I think Cameron got pregnant during the family reunion. The reunion was mom's family. If you're not her father and I'm not her father that leaves Justin."

"Son, your brother's gone. And losing him and your mother helped me to really understand that all we have is family—,"

"You knew." Jacob cut him off. "You knew Justin slept with my wife and you never told me."

"This is the time," his father stuttered. "But it's not the place."

Jacob heard heels clicking behind him. He turned and saw Cameron walking down the hall towards them. She was doing something to her cell phone, so her head was lowered. Her betrayal was worse than he'd ever imagined. His heart broke into a million pieces. Feeling the heat of tears stinging his eyes, his rage propelled him toward her. "I can't believe I let myself get involved with you again."

She looked shocked. "Excuse me?" Her eyes skittered between him and his father.

"I tried so hard to hate you for what you did to me. For what you did to us, but this time, I don't think it's going to be that hard. I'm pretty sure I'll get it right."

His father put a hand on his arm and said, "Jacob, stop. There's something you need to know."

"What did you say to him?" she asked his father.

"Don't you talk to my father," He growled. "He can't keep your dirty little secret anymore."

"Son!" He felt his father's touch again. Jacob wrenched his father's hand from his arm and pushed the man back. He thought about his weak heart, but the shot of pain to his own heart was too great. He shot him a hateful glare and returned his attention to Cameron. "You slept with my brother." He looked at his father. "And you knew and kept it from me?" His eyes bore into Cameron's again "I'll pay out your contract. But I never, ever want to see you again. Do you understand me? Never!" He turned to the elevator and pushed the button. He had to get out of this hospital before he hurt both of them.

"So typical of you to say your piece, pay the rent and

run away like a little boy." She oozed sarcasm.

He turned around. "Like a boy. Is that what this about? I wasn't man enough for you?"

"You're not being man enough right now," she retorted.

He stepped closer and put a finger near her face. "I'm man enough to have the sense to leave before I kill one of you."

Cameron slapped his finger away. "I didn't sleep with Justin."

"My brother was AB negative. We all are and so is Charity. She has his eyes for Christ's sake or hadn't you noticed that? They're his eyes, my eyes, and my father's eyes. So it was either my father or my brother." He crossed his arms over his chest. "My father says he ain't the baby's daddy, so now you tell me who does that leave?"

"Jacob," his father's voice was firm. "This is a public place. Please, let's all go some place private and discuss this."

He shot his father an icy glare. "Private." He laughed manically. "There's nothing private about her. She's a media whore. Isn't that what they call it?" He looked at Cameron and sneered. "A whore all the way around."

"Your brother raped me." The words spilled out of her mouth so fast he wasn't sure he'd heard them all correctly, but there was one that had come through crystal clear. *Raped.*

'What' was on the tip of Jacob's tongue but before he could utter it she continued.

"He raped me in your father's guest house during the family reunion." She turned and looked at his father. "And your dad wouldn't let me call the police. He convinced me that no one would believe me, that you wouldn't believe me. That we were family and family didn't lock each other up.

So, I took a shower and tried to forget about it and I was doing kind of okay with that, until I found out I was pregnant."

The wind left his body. Jacob had experienced the feeling playing sports. Once, he caught an elbow in the chest, he thought he'd never breathe again, but getting hit on the field did not compare to this. He fought to breathe before he spoke. He looked to his father. "Dad."

The elevator door opened. Hospital security approached them.

"Can I ask your party to take this conversation out of the corridor?" the young man said.

Jacob could see the shame of the truth on his father's face.

He looked at Cameron. Her disgust was palpable.

"This is my daughter's room," she said to the security guard. "Her grandfather can stay, but that man…" She pointed at him, "…is no longer welcome. Ever."

She pushed the door to Charity's room open and disappeared behind it.

# Chapter 29

Cameron gave her daughter one last squeeze, kissed her mother, climbed into the rental car and headed to the airport. Charity was better. Her arm was still in a cast, but Cameron promised her she'd be back in a few weeks when it was time to take it off. She was also planning to stay for awhile to get her back and forth to physical therapy and in general, nurse her back to health. Because before the next school year began, Charity was coming to New York to live with her.

In the meantime, the show had to go on, so she had to get back to New York. Cameron had taken a five a.m. flight because she was determined to do something she hadn't done in months. She pinned her hair up under a hat, donned a large pair of opaque sunglasses, and went to church.

She loved church, or at least she'd loved it prior to becoming Cameron Scott, the celebrity. Now she spent more Sundays than she cared to watching her pastor streaming on the internet. Fame had its costs and one of them was the lack of privacy even in the house of the Lord. She couldn't worship in peace. People recognized her, wanted her autograph, snuck and took pictures of her, asked to take pictures with her and in general paid more attention to her than they did to the message. It was invasive and it took away from her ability to relax and enjoy the service, but no matter what, this week she was going to push her way. This week, she wasn't going to let her fans and foes stop her. This week, she wanted to feel the music. She wanted to worship in God's house, so that determination ordered her steps.

She entered Higher Living Christian Church about forty minutes before the service began and claimed a seat midway through the sanctuary. She took out her cell phone and pulled up the selfie she'd taken with Charity and stared at her child until tears welled in her eyes. She'd always looked at Charity and seen the features that reminded of her Justin Gray. Those hazel eyes that were more yellow than brown, the broad nose and square jaw. But now she saw her mouth, which included naturally pouty lips and her forehead. She had her forehead. Cameron saw less of Justin's features and more of her own. Charity was starting to look a little like her and she wondered if the girl had always looked a little like her. She wondered if she'd been looking at her daughter through lenses filtered with the pain Justin had caused her. She put the phone in her purse and reached for Kleenex. She wiped the tears that had begun to spill. Her heart was so heavy. She loved her daughter, but she realized the distance between them was not just miles. And the miles were not just about her work. She'd allowed Justin Gray to take something else away from her. She'd allowed how she felt about him to affect how she felt about Charity and for that she audibly and heavily cried.

After a few minutes, she felt someone nudge her shoulder. She looked up and saw Stacy standing there. She was dressed in the green and white uniform the church greeters and ushers wore and she was holding a box of facial tissues in her hand. "Looks like you're going to need these."

Cameron stood and hugged her friend, long and hard. When they released each other, Stacy said, "Pastor Ivy saw you weeping and crying over here. She wants to see you after service."

Cameron looked toward the pulpit and saw the associate pastor, Ivy Henson. Pastor Ivy, as she preferred to be called, was kneeling before her seat in prayer.

"Can I tell her to expect you?" Stacy's voice pulled her

attention back to her friend.

Cameron let out a long cleansing breath and responded, "Why not."

"I've got to go. Let's have brunch after you finish meeting with Pastor." Stacy went off to attend to her duties.

Cameron reclaimed her seat. The sanctuary was nearly full now. She looked up at the pulpit. Pastor Ivy nodded a hello to her. Cameron smiled a little and nodded back. Pastor Ivy raised her fingers to her lips, kissed them and patted her chest over her heart. This was a code that Pastor Ivy used to remind her special parishioners that God loved them. It also meant that they were the righteous that the word spoke of in Psalm 1, and that in Christ, His beloved would never want for anything.

Worship was as it always was at Higher Living, electric and magnetic. But more important than the quality of the fine voices and the trained musicians was the Spirit that moved through the house. Cameron didn't know if everyone else felt it, but she knew she did. God had visited them this morning. She felt connected to Him in a way that she hadn't in years.

The senior pastor approached the podium and stated, "We're going to go right into the message. Check the church app, or the website or your email for events and let's get to the word that God has given me today." They were instructed to open their Bibles, or tap on their electronic versions until they found the scripture for the text.

\*\*\*

After service Cameron entered Pastor Ivy's office and took a seat in front of the woman. She remembered the first time she'd met Pastor Ivy. It was shortly after she'd moved to the city. She'd been having a hard time. She was unemployed, quickly going through her savings and trying desperately to stay sober in the midst of her problems. She attended AA meetings at the church, which was where she met Stacy. Stacy, a product of two alcoholic parents had begun drinking at the age of twelve and entered treatment the summer before she attended college. She had been dry for nearly ten years. Cameron was drawn to her and then drawn to Higher Living because of Stacy. Eventually, she'd found her way to individual counseling through the women's ministry of which Pastor Ivy was the ministerial charge.

"It's good to see you, Cameron." Pastor Ivy began. "I'm glad to see things are working out for you on the show. I enjoyed the episode with Hunter Perry and I look forward to watching this summer."

"Thank you, Pastor Ivy. The season is filled with powerful stories. I think I learn something from my guest every week."

"Something about forgiveness," Pastor Ivy stated. She always got right to the point, which was something Cameron liked and disliked about the woman.

Cameron shrugged. "I guess so."

"Second chances are about letting go of the past and trying again. In order to let go, we have to forgive something, forget to the best of our ability what happened before and make a commitment to the new opportunity."

Cameron nodded. "I understand."

"You were weeping pretty hard before service. Please tell me what's got you so brokenhearted."

Cameron took a deep breath and said. "Everything."

Pastor Ivy raised an eyebrow and repeated Cameron's word. "Everything." She sat back in her chair. "Well, let's start at the bottom. Let's start where we left off the last time we had a session."

"You can remember two years ago?"

"God brings everything I need to know back to my remembrance," Pastor Ivy said. She lifted a folder and waived it. "Plus, I have a paper file."

They both laughed. Then Pastor Ivy's tone took on a serious quality. "We were working through the pain of the rape. I have a feeling that if everything is wrong, you stopped working when you stopped coming to see me."

Cameron thought she had cried all the tears she could produce in a day, but she hadn't. She started up again. She'd been avoiding the pastor's eyes as much as possible, but this time she looked directly in them. "I've let Justin Gray destroy everything in my life." Cameron reached into her purse and removed the envelope David Gray had given her. "I went home a few weeks ago. My daughter was in an accident."

"Oh no." Pastor Ivy's concern was foremost. "Is she okay?"

"She's great. She was hit by car and she had to have surgery to repair a broken arm, but she's a trooper. She's back to herself." She swallowed. "When I was home, I saw Justin's father and he gave me this letter. It's from Justin. I told you he died, but I didn't know he'd committed suicide until his father shared that with me during my visit."

"Tell me about the letter."

Cameron shrugged. "I haven't opened it yet."

Pastor Ivy frowned. "Why?"

"I don't know. I guess if he killed himself maybe he was looking for forgiveness," Cameron replied. "Or maybe it's the final knife in my heart. Maybe he said something cruel. I can't seem to make myself read it."

"What do you really think is in it?"

Cameron felt the salty taste of tears in her mouth. It was hard to breathe. If she didn't know any better she'd think her heart had literally split in two in her chest. She shook her head. She couldn't speak.

Pastor Ivy leaned forward in her seat. Her eyes pleaded before she opened her mouth. "Please allow yourself to forgive him, Cameron. Forgiveness may start with the words on that paper."

"What if it's the opposite? What if he was just being evil and said evil things? What if he called me a whore again?"

"Are you a whore?" Pastor Ivy asked. "Do you believe that you're what he called you?"

Cameron swiped at her tears. "I never talked to you about this, but Kirk is a small town. It was really small when I was growing up. My mom was known to do things for money you know, with men. I don't know if I'd say she was a prostitute, but there were lots of men. Lights that were off came back on and food appeared in the refrigerator." She closed her eyes to wash away the memory of the men coming and going. Cameron hated to talk about this. She'd tried so hard to shut it out. She opened her eyes. Pastor Ivy was waiting for her to finish her story, so she swallowed and continued.

"My father was a married man. He never acknowledged me. Once I was in the store with my mother and he greeted her, but he didn't even look down at me. It was like I wasn't there." She paused. "And my mother's father was a married man too." She avoided Pastor Ivy's eyes for a moment. "Scott women have always kind of had a reputation for being loose. My mother's father was the former mayor. His wife had been sick…it was a scandalous situation and it seems to have followed us for generations. That's why I try to work so hard. I don't want Charity to grow up under that."

"So, being called a whore has a bit more meaning to you?"

"It's like my legacy." She paused again. "When Justin forced himself on me I felt like I deserved it. Like I had been living some kind of fantasy with Jacob. It was like his brother threw a bucket of ice water on me and woke me up from my dream and reminded me of who I was, because he could see the Scott truth on me."

"Cameron, baby, your mother and your grandmother's sins aren't yours."

"They shouldn't be, but sometimes I look in the mirror and I hate what I see. I feel dirty all the time."

"The devil always knows what to use." Pastor Ivy shook her head. "Sweetheart, you can't be dirty and washed in the blood of the Lamb at the same time. How does Jesus fit into all of that? If you're caring the burden of your family's mistakes, how has the Son of God set you free?"

"I don't know. Maybe I'm not really saved."

Pastor Ivy shook her head. "Oh no, we're not going to do that. Not in my office. Not in here today." She tapped the nail of her index finger on the desk and said, "Let me tell you this one thing I know. Nothing can separate you from the love of your God. You just have to work on Romans 12 and renew your mind. You have to take control of your thoughts and bring every one under submission to God's will. You'll never forgive Jacob if you don't first forgive Justin and stop letting the devil tell you who you are."

Cameron put the letter on the desk, buried her face in her hands and let the scriptures Pastor Ivy quoted circulate through her mind. Then she looked up. "Would you please read it first? Make sure it's okay for me to allow what he said into my head?"

Pastor Ivy nodded. Removed the letter from the envelope and began to read silently. When she finished she stood and handed the letter to Cameron and said, "Baby, you need to read this for yourself."

# Chapter 30

Jacob wanted the throw his phone out the car window, instead he banged on the steering wheel. He was minutes away from the restaurant where Cameron and Stacy were having brunch, mere minutes away from his and Stacy's planned arrival at the women's table where Stacy would excuse herself to the restroom and never return so he could have some face time with Cameron. It was a good plan, but apparently it had backfired. Stacy texted him with notification that Cameron was not feeling well and she'd left the restaurant already. That's what he got for being sneaky…nowhere.

Stacy had told him Cameron was at service, but he was already at church with Ethan and Deniece. He didn't want to be rude and leave. Besides, he and Cameron both needed the word God had for them this morning, so playing games in church was not something he was even trying to do.

Traffic was light. He pulled his SUV over to the side of the street and dialed Cameron's number. It went straight to voicemail. Not seeing her was driving him insane. Their last conversation made him ill. He'd called her a whore again. He swallowed his disgust at himself. Whore. His father's words. He'd grown up hearing it every time his father wanted to call some woman he deemed impure out of her name and he was surprised at how often it surfaced and spilled out his own mouth when a woman pissed him off. He closed his eyes. She'd never forgive him. Why should she?

He sighed deeply and closed his eyes. It was going to take some prayer to fix this mess he'd made. But before he could expect God to make it right for him, Jacob had to repent and let God know how wrong he had been. So this time when he closed his eyes, it wasn't to beg for his wife back, it was to repent.

"Lord, please forgive me for calling one of your children that name. I had no right to call her anything other than what you call her. Please help me to never say or think it again. Forgive me and help me to forgive myself." He prayed a bit longer and when he was done, he picked up his phone and sent Cameron a text message. The contents simply said, "I'm sorry." He looked back through his phone's text message history and counted the times he'd sent that same message. Thirty other times. Thirty times with no response.

He drove to her apartment building, parked and attempted to get in.

"I know she's here," he said to the doorman. "She's not feeling well. Would you please knock on her door and make sure she's okay?"

"Sir, I can't disturb Ms. Scott just because you want to see her," the doorman replied. "I'm sorry, but I'll give her the message that you were here, AGAIN. I'm going to have to ask you to leave now."

Jacob climbed back into his vehicle. Instead of going to his apartment, he decided to go to the office. Maybe he could get some work done. That was wishful thinking. He had been sitting behind his desk for hours. Work wasn't the distraction he hoped it would be. All he could think about was the time he'd spent with Cameron in Niagara Falls. That time they spent together had been everything. How had he messed this up so badly?

He sighed and tried to refocus. He had footage to review, guest spots to approve and a budget meeting with the TCT people to prepare for, but he couldn't focus on anything but Cameron. He dropped his head in his hands. He'd broken her heart, twice. Five years had passed and he hadn't done anything any better. Yelling and not listening was exactly what he'd done before. Jacob had blocked the memory of their last conversation over the years. Now he vividly remembered that time.

He'd been gone, working on a documentary in Gambia, Africa, for nearly three months. The brutal rainy season had stopped the filming. He had a week before he had to be back on the set. He missed Cameron so much on some days that he could hardly breathe. So he decided to take a trip home. Even with the forty hours of round trip flight time, Jacob would still get to be with his wife for five days and to him that was worth all the effort.

He arrived while she was at school, stopped by her favorite restaurant for take-out, then the florist for her favorite roses to set the atmosphere in their apartment. Rose petals from the door to the bathtub and then back to the bed, a candlelit table and music. It was perfect.

Cameron squealed with delight when she walked in and found his jetlagged body asleep on the sofa, but he recovered quickly. The food got cold as they reconnected with each other and made love all night. Cameron cried a few times, but told him it was because she was happy to see him. Those were the sweetest five days of his life.

Then he was gone again for another month and this time the homecoming wasn't so sweet. Jacob had wanted to surprise her again, but the surprise was his. He'd found paperwork from a local clinic on the kitchen table. Paperwork that confirmed Cameron was pregnant. At first he was excited. It was unplanned, but he loved her. His beautiful wife was expecting. They'd always used condoms, but still, pregnancies happened. Then he realized she was eleven weeks. The math did not add up. Eleven weeks was not a month ago. Eleven weeks went back to mid summer.

Jacob remembered trying to convince himself that the numbers he was looking at couldn't be right. As he held the paperwork in his hand, excitement turned to heart clutching fear. He rifled through the pile of papers some more and found a pamphlet about abortion. Fear turned to dread and then dread to rage.

His anger sent him to the computer. Jacob clicked on the keyboard for over an hour where he learned about things like last menstrual periods, windows of conception, implantation and all the other words that connected the dots. He tried different websites, but with each new site he checked, his worst fears were confirmed. Still he didn't want to believe it. Perhaps the clinic had made a mistake.

Cameron arrived home. She stood in the door staring at him like he was a mirage.

"Gray," she said, but she wasn't as excited to see him as she had been the month before. Cameron's eyes weren't bright and shining. Her face was sunken and gaunt. She looked depressed. It was then Jacob realized everything he'd just learned while Googling around was true about times of conception. There wasn't a mistake. Cameron was eleven weeks pregnant. She'd conceived in the beginning of July. She'd conceived when he was four thousand miles away. It wasn't his baby.

"You're pregnant," he said. "Eleven weeks."

Cameron dropped her backpack and handbag on the floor. "Gray, I'm so sorry."

He snatched back his head. "Sorry. Are you serious?"

Cameron's lip began to tremble. She shook her head and began to cry. "I have something to tell you. I should have told you the last time you were here, but I didn't want to hurt you."

*Something to tell him. Didn't want to hurt him.* "Tell me this is all wrong," he said. "Tell me the math I'm doing is messed up. Tell me you didn't have sex with someone while I was gone."

Cameron dropped into a chair and began to sob.

"And then you, the woman I thought was a good Christian is planning to go have an abortion. I mean, I may be greasy on some of that Bible, but thou shalt not kill is one of the commandments, isn't it?"

Cameron didn't say anything. She couldn't stop sobbing.

"Who are you? Who am I even married to?" He paced in circles for a moment. When he stopped he picked up their framed wedding picture and threw it. Cameron flinched, but continued to cry. It irritated the heck out of him. "Why are you crying exactly? I should be the one crying. I just found out I married a whore."

She raised her head and locked eyes with him. "What did you just call me?"

He didn't waste time repeating it, but this time his tone were more definitive. "I called you a whore."

She stopped crying. A blank expression came over her. Cameron just sat there in the chair, no longer crying, no longer talking. That made him even angrier. He remembered moving in a blur. He went to the bedroom and grabbed a few of his favorite things from the closets and drawers, threw them into an empty suitcase, retrieved the one he'd arrived with and put both at the door.

Cameron came out of her trance. "Where are you going?"

"Away from you," he said. He removed his checkbook from his backpack and wrote a check for what he surmised would be a year's rent, pushed it to the center of the table and stood.

Cameron was on her feet too. She rushed to the door and stood in front of it. "Please don't leave. I need to tell you what happened."

He pushed her aside. "Save it. I know where babies come from." Sloppily dragging his bags behind him, he walked through it.

"Gray!" Cameron shrieked. "I can explain!"

"No, you can't and I need to leave before this sinks in and I end up in prison." On the steam of those words he ran to his rental car and jumped in.

The next day he was on a flight back to Africa. He turned off his cell phone. Closed his email account and disappeared from the face of the earth.

Jacob sat back in his chair and dropped his head back against the headrest. If only he'd had the courage to hash everything out five years ago, neither of them would have been in this pain. If he hadn't run away and cut himself off from everyone he wouldn't have spent all that time alone. But he knew why he'd run away like a heartbroken teenager…his pride. She'd been with another man and Jacob couldn't imagine what she could say that would make him feel better. He did know one thing, if she had told him about Justin, he might have killed his brother. The scripture "All things work together for the good," came to his mind. Ethan was always saying it. He wondered if all things actually had, because he wasn't in prison.

He reached for his phone and placed a call. When Ethan answered on the other end, he said, "I know you're probably sick of me, but I need your help. I need someone to talk to."

\*\*\*

Jacob spun and charged down court. Ethan gave chase and nearly caught him as he went up to the hoop, extending his body and arms and slammed the ball inside the rim.

Jacob landed on his feet, but not before slamming into Ethan and causing them both to hit the ground.

They growled and rolled away from each other.

"I'll take my hundred bucks back," Jacob said.

Breathless, Ethan replied, "Barely." He removed the folded bill from his pocket and put it in Jacob's hand. "If you weren't afraid to go to twenty, I'd beat you."

"Says the guy who just lost." Jacob laughed.

The metal door to the inside squeaked and opened. Ethan's wife, Deniece stepped out. Stiletto heels clicked on asphalt as she made her way to where they were sitting. She leaned over and offered Ethan a hand. "You are a sweaty mess."

"You know you like me that way." He winked. Deniece pursed her lips and tugged a little. He pushed the rest of the way to his feet. Jacob followed suit. "I'm down a hundred dollars."

"Is this the same hundred dollar bill you guys have been passing back and forth for three years?"

The two men looked at each other and nodded. "As long as there's another game for us to play, we'll never go broke, honey," Ethan replied.

Deniece raised an eyebrow and put her hand on her hip. "Well, we may not go broke, but my dinner will get cold if it has to wait on you. I'm going to put it on the table. Please come in and clean up." She turned and walked back into the house.

Jacob and Ethan followed. They cleaned up as they were instructed. Ethan and Deniece gave him a quick tour of the new house. Deniece served a dinner fit for a king. Then she returned to the kitchen for dessert.

"This place is massive for the city," Jacob commented. "I know it set you back a coin."

"Don't remind me," Ethan said. "It's an investment or at least that's what I let my pretty wife tell me when I wrote the check. Anyway, we'll need it in about seven months." Ethan's smile was wide.

"Man, for real? You two are pregnant?"

Ethan laughed. "My wife's pregnant. I'm along for the ride."

They bumped fists as Jacob said a hearty, "Congrats, man!"

Ethan raised a finger and shushed him. "Deniece is a little superstitious. She doesn't want me to tell anybody until she's out of her first trimester."

Jacob threw up his thumbs. "Mums the word, for real."

Deniece came back out on the balcony with two slices of pie, bottles of water and cups of coffee. She eyed them suspiciously. "What are you two talking about?" she asked handing one to each of them.

"We were talking about how fine you are," Ethan replied.

She rolled her eyes. "Smart aleck. I'm going let you have him, Jacob. I have work to do. Before I go, can I get you anything else?"

"We know how to find the kitchen, but you can hook me up with some sugar," Ethan teased as he pulled her into his lap and kissed her, long and hard.

Jacob cleared his throat. "Can we break that up? Some of us aren't gettin' no sugar."

Deniece laughed and stood from Ethan's lap. "I'm starting to think your friend is an exhibitionist. There's something about this balcony." She walked back through the door and Ethan yelled after her. "That's right! I want the entire world to see how much I love my wife."

The men chuckled and raised forks to the key lime pie.

"So," Ethan began. "Let's get to the point, bruh. What's going on?"

Jacob filled Ethan in on the mess he'd made of things in North Carolina. When he was done, Ethan whistled low and hard. "Now that's a story."

"I've already beat myself up about it and I can't redo any of it, so…"

"So aside from being wrong about everything, what else is going on? Are you tripping on your brother?"

"I'd be lying if I said I wasn't. He wrote me a letter. Apologizing. Telling me he was sick and depressed. Jealous of me, of all things." He shook his head. "I'm still trying to forgive him, but it's hard to forgive a man you can't punch in the jaw."

Ethan chuckled wryly and cocked an eyebrow. "I agree with that."

Jacob looked in his friend's eyes. He wanted answers so badly. He needed Ethan to say something that would make him feel better.

"There's more?" Ethan asked.

"Yeah, there's more." He shoved a piece of pie in his mouth. Chewed and swallowed as he delayed the inevitable point of admitting his own failure. "She was my wife and I let her down."

"You were halfway around the world when it happened."

"Yeah, but she was my wife." He cocked his thumb at his chest. "Taking care of her was my job."

Ethan dropped his fork and wiped his mouth. "I hear you man, but you weren't there."

Jacob put down his fork too. His appetite for the pie was ruined anyway. He sighed deeply and shook his head. "I should have been. We were newlyweds. She didn't know my family. It was my idea for her to stay in the guest house. I insisted she go to the reunion. She didn't even want to go without me."

"Jacob, you're being too hard on yourself. Your brother committed a crime, not you."

"I should have passed on the project."

"There was no way for you to know your brother would do what he did."

"I should have known," Jacob stated, shaking his head. Guilt seeped into his pores. He was sure Ethan could see it in his eyes. "I don't think it was the first time, E. I've spent a lot of time rehashing the past in my mind. I don't think Cameron was the first woman Justin raped."

# Chapter 31

Cameron opened the door. Stacy handed her a brown paper bag and rushed past her in a frenzy.

"Girl, you got me running all over town trying to find some Red Rock." Stacy dropped her handbag, collapsed on the sofa and kicked off her shoes. "That must be some stuff they sell in the country, because don't nobody in this city know anything about Red Rock Ginger Ale."

Cameron put the bag on the table and removed a four pack of some ginger ale she'd never heard of and a box of organic ginger tea. "What made you buy this? I hate ginger tea."

"Ginger is good for digestive issues. I went to Whole Foods and that's the best real ginger-ale on the market because it actually has ginger in it. As for the tea, like it or not, it's probably even better for you because it doesn't have all that sugar in it."

Cameron pulled one of the bottles from the carton and placed the other three in the refrigerator and joined Stacy in the living room. "I'm feeling a little better. I appreciate you trying to help me." She popped the cap off the bottle, took a long drink and grimaced. "That's got a bite."

"That's the ginger. It'll help, I guess. That is if you have the stomach flu."

Cameron put the bottle on a coaster. "It's been a few weeks and it's on and off so I'm starting to wonder if it's my nerves."

Stacy reached into her handbag and pushed a small brown bag across the table. "It could be your hormones."

Cameron squinted and reached for the bag. She opened it and removed the contents. "A pregnancy test."

"Stomach flu doesn't last this long and if your nerves didn't have you throwing up when you were two days past homeless, they sure don't have you sick now. When was the last time you had your period?"

Cameron felt her stomach drop for real this time. She picked up her phone and pulled up a calendar. Her eyes bugged. "Oh no. I can't believe I didn't realize I missed my period. It was due over two weeks ago."

"I knew it."

"How did you know it? I didn't even tell you I had sex with Gray."

"Girl, please. A weekend in a romantic setting with that fine man, even I would have given it up." Stacy laughed. "And I don't know what you're being all secretive for. He's your husband. I'm your girl, I would have celebrated with you and been glad one of us got some."

"I was wrong to have sex with Gray. Marriage is in the heart. If you're not married in your heart, you're not married."

"Girl, that's some crap. If marriage was just in the heart then every person that felt like they were out of love would have a license to cheat. Where'd you hear that?"

Cameron shrugged. "I don't know. I've just always thought of it that way."

"I think you mixing up a sermon pastor preached. He talked about divorce beginning in the heart. You're still in love with Jacob and he's still in love with you. No one has filed those divorce papers, so you are still that man's wife.

You owed him that hit."

Cameron rolled her eyes, dropped the test on the table and pulled her feet under her bottom.

Stacy clapped loudly. "No, Ms. Thang. You rise up and go take that test."

"I can't. If it's positive I'm going to hang myself." She dropped her head in her hands. "I feel like I've been raped by another Gray man. I feel like I've been trampled on and left pregnant again. How could I let this happen to me again?"

"First of all, you haven't taken the test yet and secondly, Jacob did not force himself on you."

"Didn't he? He took me on that incredible date. He did everything in his power to create the right atmosphere to get some booty."

"So, that's called seduction, boo, not rape and you wasn't feeling used until I dropped that test on you."

"Gray men have their ways."

"Humph, if the Gray men are your enemies then why are you letting Charity see her grandfather? If any Gray was worse than Justin, it was him. So how can you forgive him and not Jacob?"

Cameron snorted her disagreement. "You didn't hear what he said to me at that hospital."

"He didn't know the truth."

"He didn't let me tell it either."

"You're blowing some of this out of proportion. Charity is clearly related to them and she does have their blood type. An extremely rare one might I add. What was he supposed to think?" Stacy dropped her head in her hands. After a minute, she lifted her head and continued. "Cam, I want you to ask yourself a question and I really mean think about this. What are you really doing here? You can't make Justin pay, so are you making Jacob pay for what Justin did to you? Does a Gray man have to pay and any Gray will do?"

Stacy's words were like a wrecking ball, knocking down all her walls and crumbling her defenses. She closed her eyes. She saw Jacob's face. The look in his eyes when she'd called him a boy. He hadn't been the only one who said hurtful words that day. She knew that would cut him to the core. Some of this was her fault. She should have told him before. None of this would have ever happened. But she'd been afraid. She'd let Justin have too much space in her head.

*"There's no point telling anybody about this," he'd said as he refastened the button on his jeans. "My brother may have married you, but blood is thicker than poon. He'll definitely take my word over a little whore like you."*

Cameron squeezed her eyes closed. "Liar," she mumbled the word under her breath, but she screamed it in her head. *Liar.*

"You aren't cracking up on me are you?" Stacy asked.

Cameron opened her eyes and sighed. "No, I'm just getting the devil out of my head."

They sat there for a few minutes in silence and then Stacy said. "I think you should take the test."

Cameron grimaced. "It's best if you have morning urine."

Stacy stood and put her hands on her hips. "There are two tests in there and with all the morning sickness you've had, I'm sure you have enough hormones in your body to take it any time of day."

Cameron rolled her eyes at her friend. "I told you, I'm trying to get my head together. I had a really good session with Pastor Ivy. That test could kill my spiritual buzz."

"Being a Christian isn't about being spiritually intoxicated. Whatever Pastor Ivy and you worked out will apply to the result of that test. Plus you might need me, so I am not leaving here until you pee on that stick."

Cameron stood, picked up the test, walked into the restroom and closed the door behind her. She followed the instructions. Then she sat on the side of the tub and waited for the results. Five minutes was all she needed, but Cameron already knew what they were. Her cycle was never late. She could set the clock by that thing.

She and Gray had made love all night. The three pack of condoms he'd had in his suitcase hadn't been enough and neither one of them had cared that they'd run out. He was such a planner. Why hadn't he had the foresight to get a six pack? She groaned.

"Lord, please, I don't want to be pregnant," she whispered. "I know that was irresponsible, but I really need to catch a break." Cameron glanced up at the ceiling like God was going to answer her. Then she stood and looked at the test stick and saw that there was a dark blue line right where she'd hoped there wouldn't be. She sighed, washed her hands and walked out of the restroom.

"Congratulations," she said to Stacy. "You have succeeded in killing my spiritual high."

"I knew it." Stacy smiled and clasped her hands together. She jumped up from her seat and gave Cameron a hug. "Cheer up. This isn't just about you. I get to be a godmother!"

Cameron guffawed. "This isn't just about me? I'm the one that's sick." A wave of nausea came over her. She bolted back into the restroom and threw up.

# Chapter 32

Jacob was trying not to quit, but it was looking more and more like Cameron Scott Gray was never going to talk to him again. They'd finished filming and editing the entire first season of *Second Chances* so she wasn't coming to the studio. He'd done everything in his power to visit her at her apartment building. If he showed up one more time, they'd probably slap a restraining order on him. He'd sent her flowers. Called her at least fifty times. He'd even gotten her mother to lobby for him and still she hadn't responded to a single attempt at reconciliation. He laughed at the karma. He'd taken off five years ago without so much as a point of contact and now here he was unable to contact her. He had this coming. He had it coming in spades.

"Are you going to sign that?"

Timothy Thompson's voice broke through his thoughts. He couldn't believe how far his mind had drifted. He sat up in the chair and looked at the contract he held. "I need to have an attorney look at it."

"You need to change your mind," Timothy said. "This show is your baby. I mean I know Phyllis was responsible for a lot of the day to day stuff, but still, you made a nice piece of change and the advertising we're lining up is good."

Jacob knew that was true, but he felt like he didn't have a choice. If he didn't leave the show, Cameron would and she needed this more than he did. She deserved it more than he did.

"No, man, I've got my reasons. The money will have to

do," he said referring to the money he would continue to earn as long as the show remained profitable.

Timothy shook his head. "Well, at least now I know why you wanted her from the beginning. She's good, but I can't believe that history, man. I'm sorry things didn't work out for you. You seemed kind of happy for a moment."

Jacob sighed. Happy for a moment. That's exactly how long it was. That's how long is always was with Cameron. It seemed like something was always happening to keep them apart, but in the end he blamed himself. He blamed his temper and his nasty mouth. He stood. "I'm going to go."

"No chance I can talk you into that other show I mentioned?" Timothy asked.

"I think it's best if I'm not around here for a little while. Maybe some other time," he offered, but Jacob knew there was no way he was subjecting himself to that. He had to get a life separate and apart from Cameron, but before he could do that, he had to figure out how to stop loving her.

\*\*\*

Jacob rushed into the restaurant. Dinner with his father was practically going to be a drive-by. His dad had flown in for a meeting and he had a plane to catch in two hours which meant he had thirty minutes before the car his father hired would be there to take him to the airport.

Jacob sat and signaled the waiter to the table. He ordered a hamburger and fries. Once the man left the table he returned his attention to this father. He looked better than he had a few weeks ago. His coloring was improved. His face was a little fuller. Jacob was sure he'd gained a few pounds. "You know I could have taken you to the airport."

David Gray waved him off. "It's on the company."

"You are the company, Dad."

"Business expenses and operating costs keep the government away. You know that by now." His father reached for the glass of water in front of him and took a sip. "How are you, son? How are things with Cameron?"

Jacob shook his head. "I'm horrible and I have no idea."

"She's still not talking to you."

"I feel like she never will."

His father's mouth twitched in a grin. "She'll come around. She loves you."

"She's angry."

"That dissipates with time." His father drank more water and then picked up his fork and began eating the salad he'd ordered prior to Jacob's arrival. "I'm going to see Charity this weekend."

Jacob raised an eyebrow. "Really?"

"Yes, I'm driving to Kirk. We're going horseback riding."

Jacob kept the sigh he wanted to release inside. He was jealous. It was durn near diabolical how things had worked out for his father. He was the one that had strong-armed Cameron into being quiet about what Justin had done to her, but at the end of the day he seemed to have the reward. "So, you arranged this with Cameron?"

His father chewed and when his mouth was empty spoke. "Cameron has forgiven me. She thinks it's good for Charity to get to know her grandfather."

Jacob fought wanting to scream again and decided to turn the focus of the conversation to the reason he'd come for dinner. "Dad, I need to ask you something and I really need you to be honest with me."

His father raised his head, swiped his mouth with the napkin and looked Jacob in the eye expectantly.

"I kind of remember something happening with Justin, but I never knew the details. I only heard parts of whispered conversations, but now I need to piece it together."

His father nodded for him to go on.

"The summer after Justin graduated from high school things were pretty strained in the house. Justin didn't go out much, which wasn't like him. Then he left in late June. He was supposed to be backpacking in Europe for a year, but even now I can't remember that being something Justin would do. He never mentioned Europe and he wasn't the backpacking type. There were never any phone calls or pictures." Jacob stopped. It was hard to push the words in his head out of his mouth. Jacob knew he was close to the truth about his brother. "There was something with a girl, the Jones family from church. Justin was dating her when I left for camp and when I came back he was gone and the Jones's well, they seemed real bitter towards us." Jacob paused. "Did Justin rape her too?"

"Your brother had a lot of problems. I'm not sure when they originated, but he really had an entitlement complex. Maybe I indulged him too much. He thought he could have anything he wanted, anytime. He was dating Meryline Jones. She was a nice girl and yes, he attacked her. He swore it was a misunderstanding. He asked me to help keep him from going to jail, so I did what I could do to save my son from prison. He would never have survived in there. I thought I was doing the right thing." His father paused. "The Jones's agreed that his going to a mental health inpatient treatment facility was acceptable to them. Ms. Jones was a single parent and well, let's just say, I wrote a large check and she took it. I thought your brother was better.

When he came back from the treatment facility he went off to school. There were no problems there."

"That you knew of." Jacob interrupted.

"You're right. None that I knew of and I assumed that year of counseling had helped him. I had no idea he still had that in him. I really thought I had helped my son, but I can see now…"

Jacob banged a fist on the table. "You could see then." Jacob's shoulders went limp. Defeated, he slouched in his chair. "Cameron was my wife. How could you let him get away with what he did? How could you not have told me?"

"I thought you'd get over her. I didn't think it would become all of this. I had no idea about Charity."

"Dad…"

"Jacob, try to understand. Your mother was fighting for her life. If she knew that Justin had done that horrible thing to Cameron, it would have killed her. I was trying to protect your mother."

"But then Mother died. I came to her funeral. What about then?"

"Tell you then, so you could tear your brother apart? My sons were all I had left and Cameron was gone. I had no idea you were still pining over her. I did what I thought was best."

"So, I suppose after Justin died it was still the wrong time?"

"I was trying to protect your memory of your brother." His father offered weakly. "I'm sorry. I made a mistake. I thought I was saving you from heartache by not telling you. I had no idea you were still in love with her. It's not like you and I ever talked."

The waiter put the hamburger in front of him. He

pushed it away from himself. "At least I don't have to wonder about Justin anymore. The things he said about women always made me uncomfortable. I thought he was just a player. I was trying so hard to admire him, but I knew…even from when we were little kids that something was off. So if I knew as a child, you knew as an adult."

"All I can ask you to do is try to understand and if you can't understand, then just try to forgive me anyway. I know it'll take some time, but we're all we have."

Jacob shook his head. He was not going to accept that. "That's not true. You're not all I have. I'm determined to get my wife back."

His father nodded. "I'm glad to hear that. She has a good heart. You should fight for her. Fight with everything you've got."

His father's cell phone rang and Jacob looked at his own. His thirty minutes were almost up. His father took the call. Once he was done, he let Jacob know his ride was outside.

"I'll take care of this," Jacob said, standing as his father stood.

"I already told them to bill it to my room." His father hesitated. "I'm sorry for all the pain I've caused you and Cameron. I'm sorry I let Justin get away with so much. If I had done something more, made him get more counseling or helped him get some medication or something… I can't help but think maybe he wouldn't have hurt people. Maybe he wouldn't have killed himself."

Jacob shrugged. "We'll never know, Dad. He might have done that in prison."

His picked up his attaché case. "We need to talk soon. I don't want more months and years getting in between us. I have a chance with Charity. She's all I have of Justin, but now I want to make peace with you. Cameron helped me to see how much I hurt you. How I belittled you for wanting a career in film. I was wrong. I'm proud of you. I mean that from the bottom of my heart."

Jacob felt his body go stiff as a board when his father wrapped his arms around him and gave him a hug. His father pulled back and their eyes met. "Have a safe flight, Dad. I promise we'll talk soon."

His father nodded and left the hotel restaurant. Jacob waited for the server and had him wrap up his dinner. He had so many things swirling around in his head at this moment, but chief among them was the fact that Justin had done this before. He knew that for sure now and it made him sick.

# Chapter 33

Cameron was sick with guilt. No matter how much she tried to shake it, she couldn't stop feeling badly about the show.

"Are you there?" Linda asked.

"Of course," Cameron replied.

"I guess I expected you to be more excited. The renewal is for fifteen episodes and your salary has been doubled."

This was good news and even better money, but it didn't matter. "I can't do it. I'm not going to take the contract."

Linda was silent for a moment, undoubtedly in shock. "What do you mean? Is there some other offer on the table that I'm not aware of?"

"There are a couple of reasons why I can't do it. First and foremost, I can't work with Jacob."

"Jacob. So you haven't heard?"

Alarm caused her stomach to drop. "Heard what?"

"He's leaving the show. Thompson will produce it next season."

"What?"

"He's leaving."

Cameron sighed heavily. Why did that make her even sadder? *Because you want your cake and you want to eat it too,* she thought.

"Cameron, I know you two have unresolved personal issues, but this is good news for your career."

Cameron nodded. Indeed it would be. In a perfect world, she'd get to keep her job which meant she could take care of her family without having to move back to Kirk and with twice the salary she could do what she'd been thinking it was time to do, put her grandmother in a nursing home and bring her mother to New York for a while. She'd already planned to bring Charity to live with her. That had been decided weeks ago, but her mother had never been out of North Carolina. She deserved to see a little of the world and New York City was a great place to start. Cameron needed the love her mother and daughter would bring into her world and then of course, there was the baby.

That was the plan if she was living in a perfect world, but she was not. Her world was on its tail. Again. There was no point delaying telling Linda why. "I know you've worked really hard for me. You've been more of a friend than an agent, but even with Jacob Gray leaving the show I still can't do it. I'm pregnant."

Linda groaned and then said, "Oh."

"I wasn't going to tell anyone until I was out of my first trimester, but I realize I have to tell you. You're in the middle of my contract negotiations."

"Who's the father? Are you still together? What's going on?"

"It's Jacob's child, but since we're not really living as married people I don't think a pregnant host is going to work on Christian television."

"No, it won't," Linda sighed deeply. "What's going on with you two?"

"Nothing, at least not anymore. It's over and I'll be

raising this baby alone."

"Does he know about the baby?"

This time it was Cameron's turn to be silent.

"Cameron, no!" Linda's disappointment reached through the phone and squeezed her heart. "You can't do this. You can't not tell him."

"Yes, I can. I mean, I'll tell him when the time is right and this isn't the right time. I need to get home and get settled and get my head completely together before I talk to him." *And my heart*, she thought. *I need to get my heart together.*

"So, you really are going back home?"

"I don't think I have a choice. My lease is up soon and this time I'd like to go before my savings runs out."

"The folks at TCT are going to be extremely disappointed. The sneak preview episode had very good ratings. People loved you."

Cameron nodded at the phone like Linda could see her. "I know. You really don't have to remind me what a big failure I am."

Linda was silent again. "You're not a failure."

"I mess up every good thing in my life, Linda," Cameron groaned audibly. "But I'm young, so I figure I can work harder to try to get it right going forward. Going home and raising my children and being a regular Jane may be it."

Linda chuckled. "But you're not regular, Cam. You've got a quality that America loves. Please, let me try to find something else for you."

Cameron shook her head. "No, I think I should cut my losses."

Linda chuckled. "I think you should give yourself a second chance and it seems that if Jacob Gray loves you enough to walk away from a top rated show then you should consider giving him a second chance as well."

Cameron bit her lip and considered how much Gray was sacrificing.

"That was your friend talking," Linda said. "Not your agent."

Cameron pushed her body deeper into the sofa cushion. "Thank you. I'll think about it."

"I'll be praying for you," Linda said ending the conversation and the call.

Cameron put down the phone. She pressed her head against the back cushion and tears the size of dimes leaked out from underneath her eyelids.

*** 

It was time to stop ignoring him. Cameron stared at the video feed to the lobby. This was Gray's fifth impromptu visit. The other times she'd pretended not to be home. She had to woman up and talk to him. He'd given up his show for her. She owed it to him to at least tell him to his face that she was not coming back, so he could.

She answered the call and told the doorman to let him in. Then she went to the restroom and wiped her face. She'd done some crying over the last couple of hours and she didn't want it to show.

Jacob entered the apartment. Their eyes locked and they had a wordless conversation with each other in the foyer. He still loved her. She still loved him. All the anger, time and avoidance in the world hadn't changed that. With their spirits they told each other so.

"I would have called first, but you haven't been taking

my calls." He stepped inside.

She nodded.

"I wasn't sure if you ignored my other visits or if it was true that you weren't home."

Cameron didn't respond. She pushed the door closed and walked into the living room. Jacob followed and they both took seats across the coffee table from each other.

"How are you?" he asked.

She tried hard to smile, but one wouldn't come through. She loved this man with every fiber of her being and everything was messed up between them. It was worse than it had been on the day he'd walked back into her life. "I'm fine," she replied. "I've been resting."

"Apparently not for the next season," Jacob chuckled, but his voice was strained. "My buddy at TCT told me you might not be renewing your contract."

She cleared her throat. "I was on the fence."

This time his chuckle was laced with disbelief. "On the fence?"

"I have my reasons."

"Cam, I invested nearly every dime I had to my name to make that show happen. I'm still not in the black. I'm not telling you that to make you feel bad, but I quit the show so you could stay. I think you owe it to me to tell me why you'd throw your career and my investment away."

She shook her head. Tears stung at the back of her eyes. "You should stay. You can replace me."

"We've renamed it. It's *Second Chances* with Cameron Scott."

"Regis and Kathy Lee are Kelly and Michael now. You can replace me."

"Not coming out of the pilot season." There was temper in his voice. He closed his eyes, propped his elbows on his knees and dropped his face in his hands for a moment. Then he stood. "Don't throw this away. I'm begging you. Separate me from the show. This is your entire career here."

"It's not as simple as you think."

"Then make it plain for me."

She didn't answer him. She was trying to figure out where to begin. She was always trying to figure out how to tell him something.

"Cam, we are done with not talking. I won't leave this apartment without the truth. You owe me an explanation, the same way you owed me one five years ago. The same way I owed you to hear you out five years ago and at the hospital a few weeks ago. We are going to talk." Jacob got on his knees in front of her. He took her hands in his. "Baby, I'm so sorry I hurt you. I'm sorry my brother and my father hurt you."

She tried to pull her hands out of his, but he wouldn't let her.

"And more than anything, I'm sorry I made you feel worse by calling you out your name. If I could cut my tongue out for it I would."

She pulled until she freed one of her hands, he was meeting her halfway, but he held on to the other and continued to plead. "I know you may not believe me or want to hear from me, but I'm sorry I let my pride get in the way of listening to you."

Cameron raised her free hand and covered her face. Tears erupted and she fought the urge that came over her. The magnetic force that was drawing her to him was so strong.

Jacob pushed his body off the floor and took the empty space beside her. He reached for her hand and pulled it away from her face. "Baby, please forgive me. Let me prove to you that I can be a better man. I can love you the way you should be loved."

Cameron watched his eyes, noting the shifting emotions they revealed...love, passion, fear and desperation. She'd seen love and passion many times before, but fear and desperation, were rare.

Quietly she said, "It's not that simple."

"I want to be a father to Charity."

He'd pulled that thought right out of her mind and it shocked her.

"I fell in love with her the first time I saw her. You know why? Because she's a part of you."

Cameron lowered her head. "She's also a part of your brother."

He cupped her face in his hands and raised her chin, forcing her to meet his eyes. "Don't you do that. Don't drop your head like you have something to be ashamed of. I don't care about Justin being her father. We were a family before my brother attacked you. We had plans and dreams and a future before he tried to steal it. I'm not going to let him or anyone come between us."

For a long time, they sat there, neither moving. Then he leaned forward, covered her lips with his, and pulled her onto his lap. Cameron lost herself in the kiss. Jacob's hands moved from her back to her head and then back across her body again. He pulled her against him so that their bodies molded into each other, just like they always did. They became one. She wanted to disappear in the kiss and surrender to her emotions. Before she lost her head, she pulled back.

"You feel it," Jacob said. "I've been questioning myself for five years. Trying to figure out if this thing between us was one sided, because I thought you'd been with another guy, but now that I know you didn't do that. You were faithful. So, I'm no longer doubting what I know to be true. You love me. You want me. You feel what I feel."

He was so right. Why was she fighting him? Was she trying to make a Gray pay?

"Baby, please, let's just love each other," He begged "Let's start over and this time we don't hold anything back."

"I'm pregnant." Cameron said the words before she stopped herself.

Confusion etched his face. "What?"

Cameron wriggled out of his arms and stood. Jacob followed her lead and did the same. "I'm pregnant," she repeated. "That's why I quit the show."

He gave a light laugh. "Niagara Falls?" His voice held a question and Cameron gave him the evil eye. "Of course. It's the only time we've been together." He looked stunned for a moment. He raised a hand to wash over his face. When he removed it a smile widened his lips. "You're having a baby."

She shrugged almost apologetically. Gray scooped her in his arms and spun her around. Cameron gasped. "Put me down or you're going to be wearing my lunch."

He stopped and lowered her to the couch. Then he dropped to his knees again in front of her. "When were you planning to tell me?"

"Soon," she replied. "Really soon."

"So, I don't get it. What does being pregnant have to do with you leaving the show?"

"The Thompson morality clause in my contract."

Jacob shook his head. "But, surely, you knew that I'd

want us to work out our marriage."

"I wasn't sure if I wanted to. Not until I saw you standing in the lobby a few minutes ago." She paused a beat. When she spoke she couldn't keep the squeak out of her voice. "I looked at you and I realized, I love that man. I love him and it's never going to stop." She touched the side of his face. "The way I feel about you is never going to go away, so I owe it to you and to me and this baby to stop being afraid to love you."

Jacob dropped his head in her lap for a moment. He wrapped his arms around her waist. Cameron could feel his lips move against her hip as he murmured the words 'thank you' over and over again.

He raised his head and reached up to sweep a fallen tendril of her hair behind her ear. "Thank you."

They exchanged a warm look. Then Jacob looked like he remembered something. He reached into his pocket and pulled out a ring box. "I have something for you." He pushed back the lid.

Cameron was shocked. She shook her head. "My rings, but how?"

"Stacy told me where you pawned them, so I went and picked them up. I was right on time too. A couple was looking at them." Jacob removed the rings. He took her left hand and slid them midway up her ring finger. "I never want you to take these off."

She smiled and waited expectantly.

"Let me make this official." He cleared his throat. "Cameron Scott Gray, if you'll give me a second chance to be your husband, all the way, not just on paper, not just for T.V., not just for ratings…I promise I will spend the rest of my life making you happy." He pushed the rings the rest of the way up her finger.

Cameron tore her eyes from the diamonds and cupped his face in her hands. "Only if you give me a second chance too."

Jacob smiled. "We're going to have reality right at home."

Cameron slid from the sofa and into his arms and whispered. "Completely unscripted."

He rolled her onto her back and kissed her like only he could.

# Chapter 34

*One year later…*

Winnie Walker's audience's applause had never been louder. She took her seat opposite Cameron. "Cameron, you know I'm glad to have you back on the show!" She looked out at the studio audience. "Isn't it great to see Cameron again?" They applauded and most of them showed their enthusiasm by standing to their feet.

"It's good to be back."

Winnie placed a hand on Cameron's forearm. "So, you've had a lot happen in the last year."

"I have," Cameron replied.

"You have a hit show, you released a book that shot to the New York Times bestseller list last week, a hit marriage, a hit family and an Emmy nomination."

Cameron laughed. "I guess that about sums it up."

"My mother used to say, 'what a difference a day makes'. What a difference a year makes, Cameron." Winnie smiled and then said, "Get a shot of Jacob Gray, Cameron's husband and her two beautiful children." Winnie pointed into the studio audience. Jacob was holding their three month old son and Charity was sitting next to him. The camera zoomed in on Jacob. "America, this is the date I got for Cameron Scott."

Applause sounded from the audience. "He's a hottie

and the executive producer for your show."

Then the camera zoomed in on the baby and Charity. "And these are her two beautiful children, Charity and Israel."

Awwws and ooohs sounded.

"You look unreal for someone that just had a baby," Winnie began. "And I see you're teasing me again with a Prabal Gurung dress. You know how jealous I get that you small women can wear Gurung."

Cameron laughed.

"You know Cameron, I think you kind of owe a little thanks to me. The last time you were on the show I got the 'Find a Date for Cameron' thing going."

Cameron sat back and braced her arms on the chair. "You did."

"But I didn't know you didn't need a date. Apparently, you just needed a second honeymoon."

Cameron laughed and looked at Gray. He smiled.

"Well, I think I'm going to say thanks for trying and give the credit to God."

"Says, the Christian talk show host," Winnie replied. "I know when to get out of the way. I'll let God have that."

The audience applauded.

"So, Cam, you've got a lot going on. You're getting behind the camera this year and directing a movie."

"I am," Cameron nodded. "I never wanted to be in front of the camera, but that's just how things worked out for me. It was easier for me to get a job on camera."

"That's because you're so gorg," Winnie said. "The curse of beauty in this industry. I'm excited for you, but now I really want to talk about this book." Winnie reached under her chair. "Unbreak My Heart." Winnie turned the book face out so the audience and cameras could focus in on the cover. "Great title. Fantastic picture of you. Tell my audience what it's about."

"It's my memoir. I know I'm still quite young to be writing a memoir, but I felt like I had a lot to say already." Cameron chuckled lightly. "Anyway, I wrote it to encourage women. In the story, readers find out about my struggles with fatherlessness as a child, I share my story about rape, how that led to alcoholism and how all those things affected me as a woman and a parent."

"I read it over the weekend and I have to say I was moved. I had no idea. You see someone like you who's so put together on the outside and you never know how broken that person is on the inside. I think your story will help many women to know they're not alone especially with rape. I don't want to give the story away, but someone you knew raped you. I think sometimes that's when women have the most guilt. We always think we should have known and we punish ourselves and not them."

Cameron nodded. "We do or at least I can say I did, but you know, this is a story of victory. It's an overcomer's story. I had to figure out how to put my heart back together and it took my faith and prayer to get me there."

Winnie nodded. "Your testimony is powerful."

"And empowering, I hope. I want women to know that no matter what has happened, no matter who hurt them or what bad choices they may have made that they can turn their lives around," Cameron said. "God is a God of second chances. He gave me a second chance and He'll do the same for anyone who wants one."

"That'll preach, Ms. Cameron." Winnie stood and began to clap. "Let the church say amen." The audience broke into a deafening applause.

Cameron looked at her family. Gray raised two fingers to his lips, kissed them, and patted them over his heart. Her own heart over flowed with love for him. The audience was on their feet giving her a standing ovation. With all the blessings God had poured into her life, she knew without a doubt that she was one of the righteous.

## The End

# About the Author

 **Rhonda McKnight** is the author of the USA Today reviewed, novel, *Breaking All The Rules*, *Give A Little Love* and *Black Expressions* Top 20 bestsellers, *A Woman's Revenge* (Mar 2013), *What Kind of Fool* (Feb 2012), *An Inconvenient Friend* (Aug 2010) and *Secrets and Lies* (Dec 2009). She was a 2010 nominee for the *African-American Literary Award* in the categories of Best Christian Fiction Novel and Best Anthology. She was the winner of the 2010 *Emma Award* for Favorite Debut Author and the 2009 *Shades of Romance Award* for Best Christian Fiction Novel. Originally from a small, coastal town in New Jersey, she's called Atlanta, Georgia home for sixteen years. Visit her at www.rhondamcknight.net and www.facebook.com/booksbyrhonda and join her Facebook reading group for discussions about her books at https://www.facebook.com/groups/rhondamcknight/

# Books by Rhonda McKnight

**Breaking All The Rules**

-Book One – *Second Chances* Series-

Oct 2013

Deniece Malcolm is shocked and heartbroken when she finds out her baby sister, Janette, is marrying Terrance Wright, because she was the one who was supposed to marry him! Everybody knows there's a rule about dating exes. Janette is pregnant and not only is this wedding happening, but Deniece has to arrange the festivities.

Deniece's feelings and pride are hurt, but surprisingly, Terrance's younger, sexier, cousin, Ethan Wright, is there to provide a listening ear and a strong bicep to cry on. Ethan's interested in Deniece, but she has a rule about dating younger men. Despite her resistance, things heat up between them and Deniece begins to wonder if it's time to break a few rules of her own.

## An *Inconvenient* Friend

Aug 2010

Samaria Jacobs has her sights set on Gregory Preston. A successful surgeon, he has just the bankroll she needs to keep her in the lifestyle that her credit card debt has helped her grow accustomed to. Samaria joins New Mercies Christian Church to get close to Gregory's wife. If she gets to know Angelina Preston, she can become like her in more than just looks, and really work her way into Greg's heart.

Angelina Preston's life is filled with a successful career and busy ministry work, but something's just not right with her marriage. Late nights, early meetings, lipstick- and perfume-stained shirts have her suspicious that Greg is doing a little more operating than she'd like. But does she have the strength to confront the only man she's ever loved and risk losing him to the other woman? Just when Samaria thinks she's got it all figured out, she finds herself drawn to Angelina's kindness. Will she be able to carry out her plan after she finds herself yearning for the one thing she's never had . . . the friendship of a woman?

## What Kind of Fool

Feb 2012

*The Wife, Her Husband. Their faith.* . . . Will it save them before it's too late, or will an enemy from their past destroy their marriage forever?

Angelina Preston tunes out the voice of God when she decides to divorce her husband, Greg. She's forgiven him for his affair, but she won't forget, even though her heart is telling her to. Shortly after she files divorce papers, she finds out her non-profit organization is being investigated by the IRS for money laundering. In the midst of the very public scandal, Angelina becomes ill. Through financial and physical trials, she learns that faith and forgiveness may really be the cure for all that ails her, but can she forgive the people who hurt her most?

Sexy, successful Dr. Gregory Preston didn't appreciate his wife when he had her. His affair with a devious man-stealer has him put out of his home and put off with women who continue to throw themselves at him. Greg wants his wife back, but he'll have to do some fancy operating to get her. When the secrets and lies from his past continue to mess up his future, Greg finds himself looking to the God he abandoned long ago for a miracle only faith can provide.

Samaria Jacobs finally has the one thing she's always wanted: a man with money. The fact that she's in love with him is a bonus, but even so, life is anything but blissful. She's paying for her past sins in ways she never imagined and living in fear that the secret she's keeping will separate them forever.

CPSIA information can be obtained at www.ICGtesting.com
Printed in the USA
LVOW01s2058140815

450229LV00006B/31/P